BUSINESS TRIP CHRONICLES

BUSINESS TRIP CHRONICLES

THE COMPLETE SERIAL NOVEL

Franco de Rocco

Franco de Rocco

This book is dedicated to my partner, confidant, and husband.

Contents

Author's Note

Please note that the text provided is a work of fiction and should be perceived as such. It is a result of my imagination and does not depict real-life events or personal experiences. The relationships and situations portrayed are purely for entertainment purposes and do not offer advice or endorse real-world actions.

However, it is important to emphasize the significance of sexual health and safety in any context. In real-life situations, engaging in sexual activities should always involve informed consent and responsible decision-making. It is crucial to prioritize one's well-being and take necessary precautions to prevent the transmission of sexually transmitted diseases.

Franco de Rocco.

1

The Bathhouse

As the airplane descended, I couldn't resist looking out the window and admiring the city below me. Despite knowing this trip involved work, the allure of returning to the "Emerald City" was too strong to resist. This visit would allow me to explore my sexuality without prying eyes—notably, that of my husband.

Every relationship has its challenges, and unfortunately, ours was no exception. Our love life had become repetitive and unexciting. To make matters worse, I recently discovered his affair with a co-worker. This discovery ignited anger within me, compelling me to reclaim what had been missing. If my husband was having extra-marital sex, perhaps I should too.

Looking at the Seattle skyline and the glistening water surrounding it, I couldn't help but notice the similarities to my hometown.

"Do you live here?"

I turned to the person sitting next to me, noticing their casual attire of jeans and a T-shirt, accompanied by a friendly smile. I replied, "San Francisco."

"Traveling on business?"

I nodded, thinking my navy blue suit and white shirt had tipped him off. He had slept the entire flight, so this was our first interaction. I raised my nose, smelling alcohol and cigarettes on his breath. Looking at his face, his mustache, dark hair, and long sideburns were a giveaway, but the leather jacket he wore confirmed it. He was queer and belonged to the BDSM community.

"I partied all night."

I replied, "Oh," not sure what to say. That explained why he slept through the flight. My gaze inadvertently dropped to the bulge in his jeans, and when I looked up, he smiled knowingly.

"Like what you see?"

My eyes widened in embarrassment.

He smirked and stared downward, checking me out in return. Seeing nothing, he looked up. "You should swing by 'The Grotto.' I'll buy you a drink."

"Is that a gay bar?"

"Yes. I'm the bartender."

This guy's coming onto me. I thought as words escaped any response.

"You're married."

I stared at him, bewildered.

He pointed at my hand. "The ring?"

"Oh... Yes."

"'The Grotto' has a backroom," he said, leaning in close. If you're looking to play..." Grinning mischievously, he continued, "I won't tell anyone."

Just as he spoke, the flight attendant began her announcement, making it difficult to hear. It was clear he knew I was gay, which took me by surprise. I didn't think I fit the stereotype.

My gaze followed his hand, making its way toward his groin. The absence of underwear left no doubt about his arousal. Even as the plane touched down and the flight attendant announced our arrival, he continued to caress himself. I wasn't sure if he was doing this for me or for his own enjoyment.

I thanked him for the conversation during our wait to disembark, assuming our interaction had concluded. However, he continued discussing "The Grotto" and how much fun it was.

He followed me into the restroom as we exited the plane. As I relieved myself, I glimpsed him standing beside me, fixated on my cock. Looking down, he wasn't urinating. I noticed the impressive size and shape of his hard-on, which stretched to around eight inches. His dick was uncut and boasted a substantial girth that left me breathless. I gasped as he continued to stroke it confidently, oblivious to the fact that others might be watching.

The excitement building within him was evident as pre-cum oozed from the tip of his cock. "What are you doing?"

"I'm horny."

Is he going to ejaculate in the urinal? I wondered.

A businessman joined us.

I faced forward, staring at the white tile wall. From the corner of my eye, I saw the businessman turning, seeing my friend playing with himself. Feeling uncomfortable and not wanting to deal with security, I quickly zipped up and turned to leave.

"Come by Saturday night!"

I didn't respond and exited the restroom, heading to the baggage claim area. "What the fuck?" I whispered and then chuckled, convinced our paths would never cross again.

* * *

The drinks I consumed during and after dinner amplified my eagerness to leave my business associates. "Enough of this," I resolved, acknowledging that I was far away from home and it was time to return to the room and prepare for my evening.

At first, I entertained the thought of visiting a gay bar but quickly discarded the idea. My desires leaned toward something more specific—a bathhouse. I had been to one before, but my concerns about contracting diseases had impeded my ability to engage. However, this time, I was determined to indulge without reservations. My goal was clear—to find a willing partner to satisfy all the repressed urges that had been growing inside me.

As I undressed, a sudden pang of guilt washed over me as I thought of my partner back home. I yearned for a monogamous relationship, but alas, it was not. Reality hit me, realizing that when two men came together, there was no standard definition of normalcy.

Letting out a long sigh, I focused on calming my racing thoughts. Despite the negativity, I affirmed I needed to do this for myself. I repeated this mantra, pushing aside the thoughts that consumed me.

Removing the douche hose from my suitcase, I made my way toward the bathroom. The shower had a convenient hand-held sprayer, a feature most people rarely use. I realized a long time ago that if you unscrewed the sprayer, you could connect the douche hose, making the cleanup process much more manageable.

As I entered the shower, I followed my usual routine to prepare myself for the night's adventures. Afterward, I stood in front of the mirror, drying off. I glimpsed my toned yet not overly muscular physique and couldn't help but find myself attractive. With my above-average height and smooth, unblemished chest, I knew I intrigued men. Inspecting my face, I realized it was time to flaunt my looks and make this evening memorable.

I opted for a comfortable shirt, jeans, and sneakers for the night. Grabbing my iPhone, I used it to map out the route to the bathhouse, deciding to walk.

I grabbed my rain jacket before stepping out, as the weather had made its presence known. The rain, though not excessively heavy, manifested as a gentle mist. Walking along the city streets, I embraced the scent of fresh air, accompanied by the swirling leaves at my feet. Taking advantage of this tranquil moment, I braced myself for the exhilarating night ahead.

I had heard about this bathhouse, one of just two remaining in the city. Its continued operation surprised me, considering the heyday of the baths had ended during the AIDS pandemic. Taking a deep breath, I attempted to push aside my fears of STDs. Even though my husband and I had never discussed extramarital sex, he suggested we take PrEP. Did he not expect that I'd question his motives? Regardless, it solidified my suspicion that he was cheating on me.

* * *

The walk to the bathhouse was brief, lasting only ten minutes. Even though the terrain was uphill, I kept a steady pace, being cautious not to exert myself.

As I approached the location, a small neon sign intermittently flashing with the words "Club Emerald" caught my eye. There were no apparent indications that this was a place for unbridled sexual activity. The street appeared deserted, with no activity. They had deliberately selected this location in a warehouse district to keep onlookers at bay.

Taking a deep breath, I pushed open the door. Immediately, the potent aroma of disinfectant mixed with eucalyptus hit my nostrils, catching me off guard. For a moment, I hesitated, unprepared for the strong intensity of the scent that filled the space.

Behind a plexiglass barrier, a man rose to greet me. He was shirtless, his chest cloaked in thick, dark hair. He flexed his biceps when he noticed my gaze, making them bulge impressively.

"Very nice," I uttered.

"Thanks," he replied.

Surprised that he heard me, my cheeks flushed a rosy hue. I coyly lowered my gaze, only to be met with the sight of his boner pressed against his shorts. It was an unmistakable sign of interest.

I raised my eyes.

"You're cute!" he teased, leaving me both giddy and slightly flustered.

As I gazed upon his dick for the second time, I let out a soft gasp. The bulge beneath his shorts now pulsated with an electric intensity. The wet spot at the tip of his cock revealed his arousal. He was a prominent pre-cummer, and the sight left me breathless.

"Fuck," I whispered under my breath. "When's your break?" I asked, my voice betraying a sudden boldness. I knew I came on too strong, but my yearning for a good time surpassed me.

His grin weakened, and he replied, "Unfortunately, I'm not allowed to play when I work."

I frowned, disappointed.

"You can come over to my place," he murmured, his voice laced with a seductive allure that sent shivers down my spine.

"Your apartment?" I replied.

He nodded. "I'm off in three hours."

"Thanks," I said, aware this seemed tempting amid uncertainty. My mind raced with thoughts of what might happen, and I couldn't help but wonder if I'd seize this opportunity if things didn't go as planned.

He handed me his business card.

I nodded.

"That'll be thirty dollars."

I handed over the cash for my admission fee and examined him. His demeanor clearly showed that he played the dominant role.

In return, he slid a white towel and a round bungee cord with an attached key across the counter.

"Have fun!" he said.

I thanked him, grateful for the meeting. I saw him admiring my ass as I exited the reception area. Returning his gaze with a playful wink, I entered the bathhouse, my heart racing with the adventure that awaited me.

Upon walking through the lounge area, a distinct sight caught my attention. Men lounged on bar stools and chaise lounges, sporting towels around their waists as they savored beverages. I couldn't help but get caught up in the room's energy as the large television screen played Robyn's "Monument" video, the beat resonating through my body.

I noticed roving eyes upon me.

"Ciao!"

Turning around, I found myself captivated by a man of Italian heritage. His powerful masculinity was breathtaking. His chest, carpeted with hair, and his professional demeanor hinted he was just my type, around my age. The noticeable bulge beneath his towel caught my attention, leading to an involuntary lick of my lips. His body was a masterpiece—chiseled and toned.

As he let his towel fall slightly, revealing his magnificent, uncut boner, I couldn't help but let out a soft gasp. His dick was thick and long, with a slight curve that begged to be explored. The foreskin pulled back slightly, revealing the glistening head.

All I could say was "shit." His hard-on left me speechless. I wanted to drop to my knees and suck him off right then and there, but I knew the lounge forbade any sexual activity.

He wrapped his towel around his waist and winked at me suggestively. I couldn't help but blush as I composed myself, hoping we'd meet up later.

I entered the locker room.

Rows of lockers adorned the walls, each one bearing a number. A pleasant blend of sweat and soap permeated the air, creating a heavy yet delightful aroma. The shower, which dominated a sizable part of the room, stood at one end.

As I approached my locker, I noticed men of all shapes and sizes. Some were engaged in conversations, while others appeared lost in their thoughts.

The sound of water splashing against the tile reverberated throughout the room.

To my astonishment, I saw an unexpected sight—two men engaged in an intimate encounter. One man leaned against the shower wall while the other man fucked him from behind. They moved in perfect unison, their bodies entwined in a passionate dance.

I moaned softly, my body's reaction betraying my longing to be in the submissive one's position. The receiver was small and slender, and the top found his ass appealing. "That's hot," I murmured, caught up in the atmosphere of exploration.

As I undressed, I kept my eyes on the man being fucked in the shower. I peeled off my shirt, neatly folded it, and placed it in the locker. I then unbuttoned my jeans and stepped out of them. The surrounding men turned as I removed my underwear.

Looking down, my prick measured around seven inches and possessed a substantial girth. My uncut cock was alluring, boasting a prominent vein that snaked its way down the shaft. I stood naked and proud for a moment before wrapping the towel around me.

It was a short walk to the shower.

I didn't need to bathe, but wanted to survey the scene and take in my surroundings.

Turning on the water, I lathered my body with soap. I washed my underarms and groin, paying special attention to my dick as I stroked it back and forth.

"Oh, my God! I'm coming!" A distant voice echoed in the background.

I looked up and saw the two men having sex in the shower. I witnessed the top experiencing his orgasm. After his body stopped spasming, he removed his dick from the bottom's ass and signaled the man beside him over.

"It's your turn!"

"Yes, indeed!" The man grinned.

The new guy didn't have any objections to being second in line and stepped forward, inserting his cock inside the bottom's ass.

"Damn! I love sloppy seconds."

The intense thrusts of the new top elicited moans of pleasure from the bottom.

A line of men formed as the scene progressed, eagerly expecting their turn. However, the man at the end seemed restless and broke away, approaching me.

I studied him closely. He was strikingly handsome and reminded me of my high school gym coach. Glancing down, I noticed the "happy trail" leading down his abdomen. His mushroom-shaped dick head was arousing, and the length of his prick was above average.

As I looked up, our eyes met, and I found myself face-to-face with him.

He gestured toward his dick.

Surprised, I hesitated momentarily, but reminded myself of my purpose for being here. I obediently sank to my knees and teasingly licked the tip of his cock, feeling it pulse with desire.

This man delighted in pleasure, so I took my time, trailing my tongue underneath the length of his shaft. As his moans grew louder, they drew the attention of those around us. Aware of the eyes upon me, I embraced the role of an eager cocksucker and started caressing his ball sack with my tongue.

"Fuck, yeah!"

Lifting my head, I asked, "Feel good?"

"Yes!" he moaned with enthusiasm.

As I continued to stroke the base, I took his dick back into my mouth and savored the taste of his pre-cum. It was unlike anything I'd experienced before. It wasn't metallic or bitter but savory, almost like a delicate fruit nectar. The taste was so exquisite that I craved more.

"Suck me!"

As I resumed sucking, I could sense the urgency in his movements. His hips thrust forward with increasing intensity, signaling his impending climax. With expert precision, I deep-throated him. As his dick head grew, he pulled out and took over with his hand.

Loud gasps accompanied his rapid strokes. "Open your mouth!" he breathed.

I obliged and waited with anticipation. Within seconds, the first stream shot out, landing squarely at the back of my throat. I moaned loudly, savoring the taste of his jizz. The second and third jets followed suit, landing on my face. I closed my eyes and reveled in the sensation, feeling satisfied.

Once his ejaculation ceased, I opened my eyes and gathered the fluid, presenting it to him.

A smile spread across his face as he recognized my reverence for his essence.

"Swallow it," he whispered.

I felt the texture and swallowed the load without hesitation, savoring its taste as it traveled down my throat. A feeling of wanting more overcame me, so I wiped the fluid from my face and licked my fingers.

The man grinned.

"I enjoyed that," I admitted.

"Thanks!" he replied gratefully.

As he turned around and left, a couple of guys approached me, thinking I'd service them too, but I politely declined by shaking my head. I knew I was ready to move on and explore other possibilities. With a contented expression, I continued bathing.

After showering and drying off, I noticed the man getting fucked again. He had already moved on to his third dick for the evening. His enjoyment of servicing men was clear.

* * *

As I entered the spacious area that housed the swimming pool and jacuzzi, the powerful aroma of chlorine filled my nostrils, causing my eyes to water. Techno music reverberated throughout the space as men lounged in the pool, engrossed in a pornographic video on the television screen.

I looked up and noticed a directional sign pointing to the "Fuck" room, "Gloryholes," and "Private" rooms.

Curiosity piqued, I started my exploration in the "Fuck" room. I followed the arrow and entered the dimly lit space. Within it, the room resonated with intoxicating moans of pleasure as men indulged in various sexual activities on platforms and slings.

I found my way to a corner of the room and became captivated by a man getting fisted on all fours. I found myself drawn to his partner's hand and arm as they delved deep inside him. The man, getting fisted, expressed his pleasure through a series of moans.

"Want more?"

Amidst gasps, the man cried, "Yes!"

The fist delved deeper.

The man's body trembled uncontrollably. I waited for a cry of pain, but he moaned even louder as the pressure on his prostate intensified.

"I'm coming!" he exclaimed and began stroking himself. Moments later, thick streams of cum shot onto the concrete floor.

"Lick it up!"

Removing his arm, the fister forcefully pushed his partner's head down, urging him to consume the substance from the floor.

"Do it now!"

The man eagerly licked up the fluid, relishing it like a delicacy. The scene mesmerized me, displaying the depths of human desire.

Just as I was about to turn away, the fister began beating off. His partner eagerly opened his mouth, ready to receive the load. The man moaned, and streams of jizz shot down his buddy's throat within seconds.

After taking a deep breath to steady himself, the man wiped his partner's face and fed him. His once authoritative demeanor faded away, and he adopted a submissive stance. The role-play had ended.

"Let's go shower," he murmured.

Now that it was officially over, I turned and scanned the room for a potential partner. My preference was to be intimate with one man—a skilled butt fucker.

Not seeing anyone alone, I left the room and meandered through the narrow hallways of the single rooms. The air was thick with the pungent aroma of poppers, and I could hear moans of pleasure emanating from the closed doors as I walked past them.

As I continued my search, I reminded myself to be open to my preferences. I had to find someone before it got too late because I had a business presentation in the morning. Turning right from the main hallway, I was in a secluded corridor. I walked to the end and hesitated, seeing the last room door open.

I cautiously peered inside.

A handsome man was sitting on the bed.

His eyes met mine, and he stood up.

As I gazed at his semi-nude body, I murmured, "Hi!" I couldn't help but notice the impressive bulge beneath the towel.

"Would you like to come in?"

I stepped into the room and closed the door. I wanted to be alone and not deal with interruptions from other men.

Turning back around, I stood, basking in the warmth of his glare. I couldn't help but feel a sense of comfort in his presence. His demeanor showed no danger or malice, and I knew I could trust him implicitly.

Without a word, he stepped forward and caressed my chest. His touch was feather light, sending a jolt of electricity through me. I let out a soft moan, unable to hold the pleasure that was building within me.

I detected his cologne scent. The fragrance wafted through my senses, a masculine aroma I recognized well—"Tom Ford."

His gaze was tender, revealing a shared longing for connection and enjoyment.

My intuition told me to remain silent and let him take the lead and set the pace. I loved being submissive, so I let him make his move.

He leaned forward and brushed his lips against mine, causing a surge of pleasure to ripple through me. I couldn't help but moan again, taken aback by his actions.

My towel untied itself and fell to the floor. Instinctively, I stepped back, reaching for it, but he grabbed my hand.

"Let it go," he whispered.

I watched as his gaze fell upon my pulsating cock, and a smile crept across his lips. He raised his head and kissed me again, his words of admiration mingling with each tender touch.

Starting at my neck, he trailed kisses to my chest, igniting a moan within me. Before I could fully understand what was happening, he slowly lowered himself to his knees and sucked me. His touch was nothing short of heavenly. He was so gentle and attentive that it felt like a divine experience.

At this moment, his actions were not driven by submissiveness but by a deep admiration for me. He was determined to show his appreciation before moving on to the next stage of our encounter.

"Can I remove your towel?" I asked, feeling a mix of excitement and anticipation.

With a warm smile, he stood and nodded. "My name's Cody, and yes, you can."

"I'm Johnathan," I responded.

I untied his towel with a mixture of nerves and desire, letting it fall from my hand onto the floor. My breath caught in my throat as I beheld his massive, uncut cock standing proudly at attention. It was thick and glistened with pre-cum. Unable to resist, I licked my lips in anticipation of tasting him.

"It's stunning!" I couldn't help but exclaim, the words slipping out before I could control myself. His response was another heart-warming smile, adding to the joyous atmosphere.

"Touch it," he whispered.

I looked at him in stupefaction.

"Go ahead," he urged.

With a mixture of awe and desire, I reached forward and lightly caressed his hardness. The girth overwhelmed me, and the firmness was reminiscent of a teenage boy. The weight of it felt massive, stirring a hunger within me. Every aspect of him evoked a deep longing.

In a breathless moment, I sank to my knees with a primal urge to pleasure him like no other. I pulled back his foreskin and exposed him in all his glory. The head of his cock produced more pre-cum. I leaned forward and licked it, savoring the taste.

As I pulled back, a string of his jizz momentarily connected us before breaking apart. The intimacy and intensity of the moment overwhelmed my senses, driving me to take him deeper into my mouth.

My display of desire only heightened his arousal, and he leaned down and kissed me.

Without warning, he gently lifted me from my knees and guided me toward the bed, his touch filled with a combination of tenderness and desire.

I watched as he sat down.

He spread his legs wide, a clear sign of his desire for me to please him. Without hesitation, I eagerly lowered myself once again.

Cody exuded the essence of a Greek God. His short blonde hair had a natural wave to it. His chiseled jawline, adorned with stubble, added a rugged charm to his appearance, while his piercing blue eyes locked onto mine with intensity. Every inch of him was like a finely carved statue, his muscles rippling and begging to be caressed. As I leaned forward, the musky scent between his legs filled my senses, further heightening my desires. His erect dick stood proudly before me, a testament to his masculinity and virility. The firmness of his ass promised a tantalizing treat for my tongue, and I longed to savor every inch.

At that moment, my cock pulsated with a fierce urgency, begging to be touched, but I resisted the temptation. My focus was on pleasuring him, knowing that my gratification would come in due time.

Pushing Cody back onto the bed, his hairy balls hung before me, beckoning me forward. I lightly licked the sack, savoring its taste and texture. As I moved toward the area between his nut sack and ass, he moaned louder, and I could feel his anticipation building.

He wanted his ass licked.

Ever so lightly, I moved toward Cody's hole. The mass of hair was astonishing. He was clean, and his impeccable hygiene was evident as I smelled it. Reaching the smooth opening, it puckered as I swirled my tongue around it.

Cody moaned excitedly.

Wanting to please him to the fullest, I slipped my tongue inside him. He raised his legs higher, wanting it to be as deep as possible. His moans grew louder and more vibrant as I explored every inch of his tight ass. My determination was to give him the best possible experience.

Closing my eyes, I fully immersed myself in his pleasure. I licked, sucked, and tongued him. Nothing was disgusting about it, and in fact, I loved it. His hole tasted heavenly, and I was its prisoner.

Lowering his legs, I returned to his boner. Running my tongue up the shaft sent him into a state of ecstasy.

He reached forward and grabbed my head, urging me to take him deep into my mouth.

I obliged him, and in seconds, his prick pulsated with desire, wanting to explode down my throat. But he stopped me, wanting to prolong the pleasure for as long as possible.

I sat back, looking up at him.

"It's time I pleased you," he whispered.

He rose and lifted me, gently guiding me onto the bed.

"Lay on your back," he instructed.

I obliged him without hesitation.

As he crawled on top of me, his weight felt heavenly, and I willingly spread my legs wide, creating the perfect fit between us. As I lifted my legs, his dick brushed against my ass, pulsating with desire.

Cody kissed my neck.

At that moment, I recognized that this man was exceptional. Perceiving my longing, I raised my limbs even higher, granting him consent. "Fuck me," I whispered to him on with my words.

The intensity of our connection was such that I became moist down below, even with no added lubrication.

Despite my protest that I didn't need it, he reached for the lube, his focus never wavering from our passionate exchange. While still kissing me, he skillfully reached for my tight ass, causing me to gasp in anticipation. With gentle precision, his finger entered me, long and thick, but with utmost care to avoid causing any pain. Next, he lubricated his shaft, preparing himself for our intimate connection.

He looked into my eyes. "Are you ready?"

I responded eagerly, "Uh-huh!" And with that, I cried out in bliss as his eight inches entered me. I felt no pain, only immense pleasure. He moved back and forth with a rhythm that approached divinity, and he never stopped kissing me, igniting my intense desire.

"Yes. Fuck me," I breathed.

Our eyes met, and my gaze conveyed my yearning for more. He smiled, understanding my desire, and fulfilled it eagerly. By making love to me with such passion, he completely engrossed me in the moment.

His kisses were intense, and he continued to shower them upon me until he finally reached his climax.

"I came inside you."

"It's fine!" I assured him, explaining I was on PrEP. My head spun. This man cared about my well-being.

"Can I suck you off?" he whispered.

He wanted me to come.

"Kiss me!" I cried.

As his tongue delved deep into my mouth, I let out a loud moan and clutched tightly onto my hardness, pumping it until a powerful jet surged forth, coating my abdomen.

Cody rushed down my body to catch the second spurt that gushed out.

"I'm still coming!" I exclaimed as two more jets shot forward. Surrendering to the intense pleasure, I kept stroking until I expelled every drop. I released my grip, collapsing onto the bed.

He returned to my mouth and fed me my cum, kissing me with all the passion he could muster. After savoring the flavor, I swallowed the fluid.

With a contented sigh, he kissed me one last time and collapsed on top of me, his weight heavy but comforting.

He fell asleep.

I gently caressed his silky locks, feeling a profound sense of contentment, as if fate had brought us together in this remarkable moment. With each joyful thought, I marveled at my incredible luck and sank deeper into bliss. Finally, wrapped in the sweet aftermath of our connection, I drifted off into a deep sleep.

* * *

I woke up with Cody spooning me, and in a daze, I smiled as I reminisced about the events of our lovemaking. As I questioned the time of the morning, I groaned. "I have a meeting soon," I muttered, not wanting to leave.

Cody sensed my predicament and rose on his elbow, disappointment in his sleepy eyes.

"It's time I said goodbye." I kissed him.

He stared into my face, and his words made me happy.

"Can you stay here just a little longer?"

I hesitated because I knew I'd be rushed, but his request made me feel wanted. "Just a few minutes more."

Taking a deep breath, I relaxed in his arms. His scent, now of sex, turned me on, and I massaged his hairy chest as he whispered to me.

"I feel comfortable with you," he said, holding me tighter in his arms.

I felt loved and secure.

Thoughts of my husband and his infidelity entered my mind, causing me to question why I had waited so long to satisfy my needs. With his comforting presence, this man felt like a gift from above.

"Can I see you again?" he asked.

Whispering, I said, "I live in San Francisco."

"Oh…"

I could sense his disappointment, so I turned to face him. Though the room was dimly lit, I could see his gaze fixed upon me. It was clear he liked me.

Determined to embrace this newfound connection, I pushed aside thoughts of my business presentation and my husband's infidelity. I'd stay in his company a little longer, even if it meant sacrificing my morning routine.

Without uttering a word, I pushed him back and mounted his abdomen. We both breathed heavily as his entire length penetrated me. Since his cum was still inside from earlier, he slipped right in. The shape and thickness of his cock's head filled me.

He grasped my hips and led me in a rhythmic motion. I gazed into his eyes as we made love. "Don't hold back," I breathed, feeling his cock head swell.

In a matter of seconds, he arched his back and released inside me.

Following his climax, I remained seated on his abdomen and jacked off. Afterward, I collapsed on top of him, my love juices cementing us together.

"I like you a lot," he whispered. His arms wrapped tightly around me.

I could see the sadness in his eyes as we both lay there, spent in the afterglow. "Do you enjoy traveling?" I asked.

"Not really."

"Oh…" I muttered, disappointed.

"But I will for you!" he replied with a grin.

I chuckled and stood up.

Cody placed his arms behind his head while looking at me. I could see the happiness registered on his face.

His jizz started seeping from my ass. I would have to use the bathroom before leaving. I wanted to keep it in, but it needed to be expelled. After wrapping my towel around my waist, I leaned forward and whispered goodbye.

"I wish you didn't have to go."

I paused, disappointed as well. Without thinking, I whispered, "Room #402. I'm at the Alexander Hotel."

Cody smiled at me.

"I'll tell the front desk to let you in."

"Really?"

I nodded. "I have meetings until 12:00. If you feel inclined, surprise me," I said, kissing him one last time and leaving the room.

* * *

As I walked down the hallway of the bathhouse, my thoughts drifted back to Cody and the remarkable experience we shared. I couldn't help but smile as I remembered the way he fucked me. Suddenly, I felt the wetness between my legs, realizing that more cum had leaked out. This served as a reminder of how thoroughly he had used me. I smirked, relishing the memory.

The bathhouse was unusually quiet at this hour—either everyone had left or was asleep. I continued toward the locker room, feeling a sense of satisfaction.

As I passed the swimming pool, a naked man caught my attention. He was looking for sex and gestured me over. I smiled and continued on my way.

The locker room was empty, so I entered a stall and went to the bathroom. After releasing his fluid, I felt saddened. I wanted to keep it inside me. After washing my hands, I dressed swiftly and left the bathhouse.

The overwhelming feeling of happiness filled every fiber of my being, radiating from a place deep within. A dormant spark inside me ignited, engulfing me in a warmth that surpassed any physical sensation. My steps back to the hotel became light and energetic, propelled by an invisible force, as if I were gliding on air.

As I entered the hotel room, I glanced at the bedside table and looked at the clock. I took a deep breath—I had time to shower before seeing my associates.

2

The Grotto

The large cup of coffee I consumed gave me the energy to get through my business meeting. Although I felt tired from the night at the bathhouse, my positive demeanor remained intact, which impressed my clients. My smile never left my face, and it drew everyone in.

After concluding the meeting, I said my goodbyes and left quickly, overflowing with enthusiasm to reunite with Cody, the man I had sex with.

Exiting the Seattle Convention Center, I emerged onto a bustling sidewalk. While weaving through the throng of people, a nagging guilt overwhelmed my thoughts. I halted, oblivious to the surrounding crowd.

"Excuse me!" a woman in her late fifties carrying a shopping bag shouted sarcastically, bumping into me.

Apologizing continuously, I quickly sidestepped and pressed myself against the building. Drawing a deep breath, I whispered, "You can do this." The prospect of crossing paths with Cody challenged my belief in monogamy. I deserve happiness, I thought, reminding myself of my husband's betrayal.

Regaining control of my emotions, I pushed away from the wall and headed toward my hotel. The clouds had graciously made way for the sun, but a chill hung in the air—a clear sign of fall.

I strolled through the grand lobby when I arrived at the "Alexander," a luxurious hotel beyond my budget. Bypassing the busy reception desk, I made my way to the elevator. Now feeling excited, I grinned in anticipation of seeing the man who had fucked me.

The lift operator, dressed in black slacks, a white shirt, and a jacket, stood inside the open door.

"Good afternoon, Mr. Cummings," he greeted in an Italian accent.

"Hello!" I exclaimed, surprised at the man's memory of knowing everyone's name.

He gestured for me to enter.

"Fourth floor."

"Yes, sir."

I should have remained quiet—he knew what floor I was on. This man was good! As the door closed, a familiar fragrance wafted through the air. "Tom Ford?" I wondered, recognizing it was the scent Cody wore. I leaned forward and discreetly smelled the operator.

"Sir?"

"Your cologne. It's very nice."

He smiled, shaking his head. "No, no, no... We're not allowed to wear fragrance. That was from a gentleman earlier."

"Oh, I see." I grinned, knowing Cody made it after all. My cock stiffened in excitement.

I looked at the operator's nameplate.

It read Matteo.

His accent, dark hair, and olive-toned skin gave away his Italian ancestry. He was handsome and exuded a masculinity that I found appealing.

Looking at his hand, I noticed no ring. "Girlfriend?" I inquired.

"Single," he exclaimed, and glanced down at my groin in surprise.

His gaze led me to notice my hard-on straining against the fabric of my trousers. Hastily, I covered myself and realized I left my wedding ring in the room. I had removed it before visiting the baths last night, not wanting to deter anyone. As guilt consumed me again, his response yanked me back from my thoughts.

"You... single too?" he inquired.

"Yes," I confessed. After a long pause, contemplating my dishonesty, I added a quiet, "I'm gay."

"Oh!" he exclaimed, tapping his chest. "I'm gay too! Where are you from?" he asked in broken English.

"San Francisco."

"Bella Citta!"

"Are you from Italy?"

He smiled. "Si."

The elevator stopped, and the door opened. He nodded and gestured for me to exit.

I stepped out and turned around. There was a moment of silence, and then I said, "Please call me Johnathan. Have a good day."

"Buona giornata."

I sighed, hearing him speaking his native tongue. It was a significant turn-on. "You're a handsome man. I find you attractive," I said.

"Grazie."

As the door closed, I realized my forwardness, but I didn't care. He was beautiful and deserved to know it.

I turned around and navigated the hallways, arriving at my suite. Standing momentarily, I took a deep breath. Inserting the card key into the lock, I heard the electronic beep. I pushed the door handle down, and the door opened.

The scent of "Tom Ford" filled my nostrils.

Letting out a sigh, I saw Cody lying naked, with his bare ass exposed amidst disheveled sheets, lost in peaceful slumber.

I shed my attire and joined him.

His sculpted backside was a sight to behold. His toned muscles dipped and curved seductively, and his round, firm butt commanded attention, stirring a deep desire within me. My boner continued to pulsate, oozing pre-cum. I couldn't help but lean forward and inhale deeply, captivated by the alluring scent of soap. He showered before climbing into bed.

I kissed his ass.

He responded with a soft moan, signaling his awareness of my presence.

Wanting to surprise him, I lowered my head and delved into his behind. The taste was unlike anything I had ever experienced, a mix of sweet and salty flavors that left me breathless. I ran my tongue over his hole, teasing and probing. His body trembled beneath my touch. As I continued to rim him, his moans grew frantic.

As his hole relaxed further, my tongue delved deeper. His hips ground against the mattress, signaling his arousal.

"Finger me," he moaned.

I inserted my finger inside my mouth and then placed it inside his ass, slowly moving in and out.

He gasped, pleading for two fingers.

I obeyed his request.

"Oh, fuck!" he moaned in ecstasy. "Stop... You're going to make me cum," he exclaimed moments later as the sensation became too intense.

My fingers slipped from him, and then I delicately licked his clean, moist hole one last time for good measure. As I pulled away, he turned over with a grin, and his eight-inch cock stood rigid, throbbing in front of me. Pre-cum oozed from the opening. I licked it, and the taste was delicious.

"Good morning!" he whispered.

"Good afternoon," I replied.

I spotted the travel-sized lube on the nightstand and recognized that he had brought it. Tearing it open with my teeth, I gathered the lubricant in my hand. "You've been on my mind all morning," I said.

I coated his uncircumcised boner.

He gasped as I caressed his hardness.

I stroked him, and the slickness of the lubrication allowed my palm to glide effortlessly up and down his shaft. "I want you," I murmured in a seductive tone.

"Hop on." He whispered with a grin.

I crawled onto his abdomen.

Grasping his cock, I lowered myself onto him. My hole was so relaxed in anticipation of getting fucked, it slid right in. "Oh," I moaned in excitement.

With his hands on my hips, we began moving in perfect harmony. With each thrust, I could feel his hardness pressing against my prostate. It sent waves of pleasure through me. More pre-cum drooled out of me.

My cock throbbed.

I stroked myself feverishly, my arousal building with every passing moment. With a final, powerful stroke, I let out a cry, and my load erupted.

It landed on Cody's chest.

Simultaneously, he let out a deep groan and orgasmed. I could feel his cock pulsating, filling me with warm fluid.

"Oh, Jesus." My eyes rolled back, and I was in utter bliss, being seeded by the man before me. I collapsed on top of him, and he wrapped his arms around me as we lay in the peaceful aftermath.

Breaking the silence, he whispered, "After you left the bath-house, I felt so lonely."

My heart swelled with delight at his confession.

"I left right after you," he explained.

"You should've come with me."

He nodded, pressing a kiss to the top of my head.

As I savored his embrace, my thoughts turned to my husband and his deceitfulness. His unfaithful behavior had led me to this point, and the intensity of my anger had driven me to cheat as well. However, after experiencing Cody's touch, I realized it was time to confront him.

Cody fell asleep.

As my eyes grew heavy, I kissed Cody's chest—a silent gesture of gratitude. As my eyelids fluttered shut, sleep overtook me. Suddenly, the phone pierced the tranquil air, jolting me from my slumber. I instinctively groped for the device on the bedside table. My heart stopped when I glimpsed the caller ID.

The screen lit up with "Brian," my husband's name.

I found myself prioritizing my happiness. Should I answer or silence the call? The ringing persisted, threatening to disturb Cody's peaceful slumber.

I slipped from the bed and headed toward the bathroom for privacy. Taking a deep breath to steady my nerves, I answered the phone, choosing to confront him.

"Hello," I whispered.

"Were you sleeping?"

"I was..."

"It's two o'clock in the afternoon."

I drew another deep breath and cast a glance at Cody. His alluring body drew me in once again. Fuck! I thought, thinking I should've silenced the phone.

"Johnathan?"

"I'm here," I said, closing the bathroom door behind me.

"What's going on?"

Taking another deep breath, I steeled myself for the conversation about his infidelity. "I know you're having…" My voice echoed loudly, and I cursed under my breath. "I know you're having an affair," I repeated.

"What?" he exclaimed in surprise.

"I've known for a while," I stated firmly, my voice wavering with anger and sadness.

There was a long silence at his end, punctuated only by his heavy breathing.

"Brian?" I pressed.

He remained silent.

I blurted out, "I went to the baths last night and met someone nice."

"You did what?" he yelled.

"He's in my bed."

Cody knocked on the bathroom door.

"Oh, fuck!" I exclaimed, feeling a sense of panic rising within me. Before I could say anything, he opened the door, looking bewildered while listening to our conversation.

I pleaded with him to remain silent.

Brian's shrill voice shattered the silence.

"Get that son-of-a-bitch out of your bed!"

"Brian, stop…"

As Brian's screams continued, Cody raised his hands above his head in anger. His expression caused my jaw to drop. Oh, fuck… This wasn't good.

"You have a boyfriend?" he asked in disbelief.

"Husband."

"You're cheating on him?"

I lowered the phone, realizing he didn't understand the situation.

"This is fucking bullshit!" Cody spat.

He pivoted and made his way toward his clothes, delicately arranged atop the chair next to the bed.

I rushed toward him as he dressed.

"Cody!" I exclaimed, trying to grab his arm, but he pushed me away.

"Why didn't you tell me you were married?" he asked, disheartened.

"It didn't come up," I replied.

"I thought you were the good guy. You're just like every other damn queer—a selfish son-of-a-bitch! I want nothing to do with you," he said, sounding betrayed.

"Cody…" I protested, throwing the phone on the bed.

"I'm not going through this again," he said, stepping into his jeans.

"Again? What are you talking about?" I asked in confusion.

"My partner cheated on me," he replied.

After buttoning his fly, he put his shirt over his head and stepped into his shoes.

"Cody, you don't understand," I pleaded.

He opened the door and shouted, "NO! YOU DON'T… UNDERSTAND!"

"Don't leave…" I begged.

He exited the room.

As the door slammed in my face, I mumbled, "Cody," not believing he was gone. I stood, feeling mixed emotions—anger, betrayal, and confusion. He left, thinking I was the bad guy. I wanted to open the door and beg him to stay, but my voice caught in my throat.

I walked to the bed, dumbfounded. I grabbed Cody's pillow and inhaled his scent one last time.

"Jonathan?" Brian's voice erupted from my phone. He was angry and demanded answers.

"Oh, fuck!" I mumbled, forgetting about him.

I threw the pillow down and searched for the phone, finding it under the sheets. Lifting it, I shouted, "What the fuck do you want?"

"Tell me what's going on."

"You cheated on me!"

"Calm down…"

"OUR MARRIAGE IS OVER!"

"Johnathan?"

"You broke my trust."

"I won't do it again. I promise."

"FUCK YOU!" I yelled, disconnecting the conversation. I turned the ringer off and threw the phone on the bed.

"FUCK!" I screamed, angry at Brian, Cody, and myself for answering the call.

A knock on the door interrupted my thoughts.

I straightened up, taking a deep breath to calm myself. Could it be Cody? Had he returned? I wondered, hurrying toward the door. I flung it open without bothering to cover my nakedness.

"Cody!" I exclaimed.

However, my smile faded as I recognized the figure standing before me. It was my friend and associate, Drew Markley.

His gaze moved from my face to my chest, lingering down to my long, uncut prick.

His eyes widened in disbelief.

"Is this a bad time?" he asked, raising his gaze.

Embarrassed, I quickly covered myself and stepped behind the door. "I'll get a robe. Come in."

Drew entered swiftly, his actions almost suggesting he wanted to see my naked body. I turned my head as I walked toward the bathroom and glimpsed him adjusting himself while checking out my ass.

He blushed.

I entered the bathroom and closed the door, seeking solace from the overwhelming situation. Retrieving the hotel robe from the hook, I draped it around my body and leaned against the wall, exhaling deeply. "No…" I whispered to myself. The man I had feelings for had just walked out, and the confrontation I had with my husband meant the end of our marriage.

"Johnathan? Is everything alright?" came the concerned voice from outside the bathroom.

Regaining my composure, I inhaled deeply and wiped away the tears. With a forced smile, I opened the bathroom door. "Everything's fine," I lied, extending my hand to shake.

Drew took my hand, his expression shifting to one of surprise. He quickly let go, inspecting his palm. Confusion painted his face as he scrunched up his features. "Is this lube?" He sniffed it, then glanced toward the bed, noticing the lube packet resting on the sheet.

"Yes."

He waited for an explanation, but I stayed quiet, shrugging my shoulders, hoping he'd drop it. "The paperwork is ready!" I murmured, changing the subject.

"Okay," he responded, questioning the entire situation. He then wiped his hand on his jeans, removing the lube.

"It's on the desk," I pointed.

I made my way toward the small table, but my clumsy movement caused the hotel phone's receiver to fall off its cradle.

"Fuck!" I muttered, freezing momentarily.

Drew stepped behind me and replaced the phone's receiver. He grasped my shoulder and turned me around, looking concerned.

"I can tell you're upset. What's going on?" he asked, his voice filled with sincerity.

"Everything…" was my vague reply.

As my robe opened, my exposed cock captivated Drew's eyes. Unfazed, he steered me toward the desk chair. Positioning himself behind me, he massaged my shoulders, helping to ease my stress.

I drew in a deep breath, comforted by his presence. We were more than just colleagues at work—being the only gay men there, we had formed a strong bond of friendship.

"Explain everything."

"Brian's having an affair."

"I never trusted that bastard," Drew spat. "I'm sorry for interrupting. Go on."

"He called earlier, and I confronted him."

"And then what?"

"It's a long story." Abruptly changing the topic, I confessed, "I visited the bathhouse last night and ended up with someone. A really nice guy. Drawing in a deep breath, I let it out slowly. "I invited him here, and we had sex again, but then he left, under the impression that I was cheating on Brian."

"Oh, my!"

Drew started massaging my chest. His touch felt sensual, making my nipples erect. After a few moments, I uttered, "I'm done with men!"

"No, you're not."

I thought deeply and realized it was time to think about myself. "You're right, Goddamnit!" Then announced, "I'm going to 'The Grotto!'"

"Is that a bar?"

"Yes... A bar with a backroom."

"For sex?"

I nodded. "I want to get fucked! Multiple times! I'll show Brian what I'm capable of..."

"Revenge isn't the answer."

I lifted my head, realizing our closeness. We were face-to-face. I could smell his scent—a masculine, musky aroma that I found intriguing.

"Johnathan?" he questioned.

"Yes," I said and followed his line of sight downward. My cock was fully erect and throbbing with blood. In disbelief, I watched as my foreskin receded by itself, revealing my glistening head. Pre-cum dripped from the slit.

"Oh, shit!" I was a heavy pre-cummer. "I'm so sorry," I said, quickly standing and covering myself.

"Fuck, dude," he breathed, impressed.

I noticed the bulge in his pants. It looked to be around six or seven inches.

A fleeting thought crossed my mind about whether he was interested in fucking ass. But I quickly dismissed this as a foolish idea. Our friendship was valuable, and I didn't want to jeopardize it for revenge. So, shifting gears, I reached over to the desk and collected the paperwork, offering it to him with a simple, "Here you are..."

"Our meeting's in thirty minutes. Are you going to be alright?" he asked, worried about my disposition.

"No..."

"Do you want me to facilitate it?" he asked, taking the paperwork.

I nodded.

"Not a problem."

"Thank you," I said, reaching for his shoulder. "You're a good friend. I appreciate you."

He drew me into an embrace. I could hear him inhaling deeply, as if savoring the scent of my hair. It felt as though he was committing every aspect of me to memory.

My cock continued to pulsate under the robe and soon snaked its way to freedom. I stepped back, and we both looked down. "I'm so sorry," I said, feeling embarrassed.

"Don't be," Drew replied, his eyes fixed on my hardness. "It's beautiful."

I sucked in a breath as he tucked the documents under his arm, then extended his hand to stroke me gently.

Closing my eyes, I felt my prick throb unpredictably under his touch. Feeling weak, I thought to myself. I've got Cody's cum inside me. I'm lubed and ready to go.

He removed his hand from my cock.

I opened my eyes.

Staring intently, he replied, "I better leave before this gets out of hand."

"Do you want to fuck me?"

Drew smiled and nodded his head.

I cursed myself that I had asked. What was I thinking? Trying to make things worse? I thought, realizing he liked me more than a friend. If we had sex, it would end in disaster. "I don't know what I was thinking... We'd better not cross that line."

Upon hearing my words, a look of disappointment crossed his face. "I guess... I'll see you later."

"Okay," I responded in a soft tone. "Thank you," I added, placing my hand on his shoulder as a gesture of our friendship.

His gaze lingered on me for a moment longer than necessary. I could sense his yearning to lean in for a kiss. I took a step back to prevent it. He offered a smile, turned, and exited the room.

The door closed.

I stood there, shocked by my behavior. "Why would you ask that? How foolish." I murmured, hanging my head in shame. Take a shower, I thought, shaking off my guilt. I took a deep breath and made my way to the bathroom.

* * *

The afternoon meeting was lengthy. I was grateful for Drew. Under his direction, the presentation was going better than expected. We made a great team, and the advertising agency back home knew it. Throughout the years, we had heard the chatter. Everyone thought we were having an affair. We laughed it off, thinking it was funny.

As Drew delivered the seminar, my mind wandered to Cody. I knew nothing about him, such as where he lived or his phone number. I realized he was now a lost soul in my life.

I caught sight of a business client from Florida stealing glances at me. My eyes widened as his tongue pressed against his cheek, giving me the universal sign of a blowjob. I turned away quickly, reminding myself to behave.

I planned my evening. The itinerary was simple. I'd get "fuck ready" and head to "The Grotto." I wanted to meet with the bartender I had met on the plane. He was the one who told me about the backroom.

* * *

I ventured toward the elevator, waving to Drew and a couple of associates. They invited me to join them for dinner, but I passed, making an excuse that I wasn't feeling well. Drew knew I was going to "The Grotto" for sex. I saw the hurt in his eyes, which cemented the fact that he liked me more than a friend. "How could I have missed that?" I whispered to myself.

I turned the corner, and once again, the elevator door stood open, and Matteo was there, smiling seductively.

"Matteo!" I exclaimed a little too eagerly.

"Please... come in," he responded.

I entered and turned around to face him. The door closed, and something compelled me to kiss him. I didn't know if it was his masculine behavior, his body, or his cock enlarging in his trousers.

At first, his eyes widened, but as I leaned in, he kissed me back, wanting it just as badly. It was sensual. The small peck turned into a French kiss.

"Oh, Mr. Cummings," he moaned, slipping his tongue deep inside me.

"Call me Johnathan."

I pulled away and gasped for air. Turning to the control panel, I slammed the palm of my hand on the "emergency stop" button, and the elevator halted with a jerk.

"No… I'll lose my job," he mumbled but continued kissing me. His arms betrayed his thoughts as he pulled me in with a passion I had never experienced. His cock throbbed against me, wanting to be set free.

"I'll hire you as my assistant if you get fired," I murmured, kissing him in return.

I caressed his boner.

"I need… to cum," he whispered.

Breaking away from the embrace, I removed my suit jacket. A smirk crossed my face as I kneeled and unlatched his belt buckle and slacks. His trousers fell to the floor.

I let out a soft moan as I admired his legs, covered in a luscious coat of sleek, jet-black hair. Tenderly, I ran my fingers along his thighs, feeling the strength beneath my touch. His cock was hard and pulsating against the designer underwear that accentuated his toned body.

"Fuck," I moaned again and reached for the elastic band, pulling his briefs down.

"Yes," he moaned, grabbing the back of my head.

His uncut cock jumped forward.

My jaw dropped. Like mine, a large vein ran down the shaft. He had extra foreskin, and his girth was meaty. The mass of black curly pubes only added to his manliness. His scent was spicy, a magnetic allure that captivated me.

He pulled my head forward.

I didn't know if he was a top, bottom, or verse, but I didn't care at this point. I pulled back his foreskin. His head glistened, and pre-cum oozed from the opening. It was heavy. He was a pre-cummer like me.

"Succhiami."

"Yes, talk Italian to me," I moaned. I didn't understand him, but it turned me on.

I licked his prick.

"Si. Si…" he moaned.

I licked the underside of his cock.

The elevator alarm went off, and the sound was loud and annoying, but I didn't stop because I wanted to swallow his Italian sperm.

"Succhiami."

I was heading for his hairy balls when he guided my head toward his dick. I engulfed the entire length of him. My eyes watered. Once I started deep-throating, I didn't stop until he started panting.

"Sto arrivando! Oh, cazzo!"

The first squirt shot to the back of my throat.

I almost choked, not prepared for the forcefulness of the ejaculation. Three jets followed, and his watery jizz started flowing from my mouth. The texture was smooth, not thick, and it tasted like pineapple. I wanted to savor it forever.

"Ingoia il mio sperma!"

I removed my mouth from his cock and looked up. I moaned in happiness and swallowed his seed. His thumb wiped the cum from my lips, inserting it inside my mouth.

"I want more."

He leaned down and kissed me.

"Oh, fuck!" I breathed, lost in his kiss.

As the telephone in the control box rang, I stood, realizing our time was over.

Matteo answered the phone in between gasps. He grinned in happiness but gestured for my silence. Then, after explaining to his boss that everything was alright, he returned the receiver and quickly dressed.

I let out a gasp as he placed his hard cock inside his underwear. I knew then that he was a multiple cummer because he never went soft. "Damn!" I murmured, reaching out one last time to feel the length and firmness. The pulsating sensation continued, and the wet spot grew bigger until I finally withdrew my hand.

"No more... Get dressed."

I put on my jacket and tucked in my shirt, knowing I needed to behave.

"Let's fuck!" he said.

I looked up in surprise.

"My break. In fifteen minutes," he added.

Matteo pressed the "emergency stop" button. The alarm stopped ringing, and the elevator started its ascent to my floor.

I stood there, admiring his beauty and savoring the taste of his cum in my mouth.

When the door opened, I kissed him and stepped out. I turned around and said, "I'll be in my room."

"Si..." he replied with a grin.

* * *

I crack the door of my hotel room before moving to the bed. Cleaning up wasn't an option, but I was confident it wouldn't be an issue. Gently touching myself, I could feel the build-up of intense pleasure. After the scenario in the elevator, I needed to unload.

I bent over the bed, lifting my ass.

Squeezing the lube on my fingers, I moistened my fuck hole. It puckered as the tip of my finger slipped inside. It felt good, so I pushed it in further. "Oh, fuck," I moaned, primed and ready for him. He could have his way with me.

Darkness shrouded the room.

Next to me on the bed, I arranged everything he would need within his reach. I took a deep breath and waited in anticipation.

"Johnathan?" he whispered minutes later.

"Come in."

The door opened, and he entered.

Remaining silent, I lifted my hips, presenting my ass for him.

"I'm going to fuck you good," he murmured in his Italian language.

I parted my cheeks.

My hole puckered, teasing him. "Use me..." I whispered, yearning to be his instrument of pleasure.

He peeled off his clothes.

His fingers probed my ass.

I inhaled sharply with intense longing. "I want your cock," I whispered passionately.

"Si!" he replied.

He lifted the open packet of lube, squeezing the fluid into the palm of his hand.

"Adoro il tuo culo."

I murmured, "I don't understand."

"I love your ass."

He lubricated his shaft and then plunged it deep into my hole. His cock filled me up completely as he started thrusting in and out of me. Our lovemaking was intense, and before we reached our climaxes, he withdrew and instructed me to turn over. I got onto my back and lifted my legs.

I stroked myself as he reentered me. My cum splattered on my chest as he ejaculated inside my ass.

After he pulled out, I crawled to the floor and eagerly licked him clean. I wanted him to know that I was submissive and that I'd do anything for him.

He dressed and then kissed me.

"I have work to do... Grazie."

I whispered, "Thank you."

"Si."

With that, he walked toward the door, leaving me breathless and yearning for more. Although I couldn't understand him most of the time, his deep voice sent me over the edge. I loved everything about him. Sitting on the floor in a daze, I relived what had just happened.

I touched myself, feeling my wetness. Raising my hand, I sniffed my fingers. It smelled heavenly, so I inserted them inside my mouth. His cum tasted good. So good that I wanted more. I relaxed my muscles, and more cum spilled out. I ate everything that flowed from me.

Afterward, I told myself, "Take a shower. You have a big night ahead of you." As soon as I stood, I stopped in thought. No... Don't clean up. I smiled. Keep his jizz inside you. Be a rebel.

* * *

The weather had deteriorated unexpectedly. The gentle mist had transformed into a torrential downpour, prompting me to pull the rain jacket hood over my head.

I strolled along the streets until I arrived at the bar. The sign perched atop the establishment proclaimed, "The Grotto." Above it, a wall of stone surrounded a cavern. Despite the sign's somewhat cheesy nature, it fulfilled its function.

Several men were outside, smoking under the awning of the establishment. They were shirtless and wearing their established leather gear. As I entered, they stopped their conversation and glanced in my direction.

"I'll see you in the backroom," I teased, flirting with them. As their eyes widened with interest, I opened the door and continued inside.

Corrugated metal panels adorned the walls, adding a touch of rustic charm to the surroundings. The bar stood prominently in the center of the room.

Men gathered in groups wearing fashionable leather garments. Some were shirtless, while others boldly sported chaps, exposing their bare asses. I turned to the bar and saw the bartender I had met on the plane. He looked just as I remembered, except now he wore his leather attire. Like the others, he wore chaps, leaving his chest provocatively bare. Nipple piercings adorned his dark, curly-haired torso, and his chaps revealed a noticeable bulge.

I couldn't help but wonder if he relied on "Viagra" to sustain his erection throughout the evening.

Walking to the bar, I waited for him to notice me. When he spotted me, he came over with a smile. Instead of extending his hand to shake, he pulled me into a warm embrace.

"You made it!" he exclaimed.

"It's good to see you!"

"Are you enjoying Seattle?" he asked.

I smiled, nodding, not intending to share anything personal with him. He was a stranger.

"Can I buy you a beer?"

"I'd like that," I replied.

He started pouring me my drink.

I looked around the room. The men all seemed to radiate an aura of dominance. They were here for one primary purpose—sex.

The bartender placed the beer on the counter. "I'm Brice," he introduced himself.

"Johnathan," I replied.

He smiled and pointed toward the back of the room. A black door with boulders painted on the wall depicting a "grotto" caught my attention.

"That's the backroom," he said.

"The door that looks like a cave?"

"Yes."

I grinned, listening attentively, thinking this was just as cheesy as the outdoor sign.

"It gets busy around midnight," Brice informed me.

Feeling thirsty, I quickly finished my beer without realizing it. My throat felt parched, and I felt grateful when Brice brought me another one. "Thanks," I said, expressing my appreciation.

"Are you going to check out the backroom?"

"That's why I'm here."

"Great!" Brice exclaimed, reaching inside his chaps. He retrieved a little yellow, round pill. "Take this. It'll help you relax and make you feel sexual."

He gave me the pill.

"It'll be our secret. Your husband doesn't need to know any-thing..."

Without hesitation, I put the pill in my mouth and swallowed. I should have questioned him about it, but I didn't care then. I was determined to fulfill my sexual desires.

Savoring the complimentary drink, I took a sip from my second beer. We continued our conversation between serving customers, and I got to know him better. I could tell he was a nice guy, and if I lived here, I'd be his friend.

Approximately twenty minutes later, I felt light-headed. My thoughts became blurred, and it became challenging to understand what he was saying.

When he glanced in my direction, he questioned if something was wrong. I couldn't respond and only grinned. He left the bar and came over to me.

"You're ready," he smiled. "Hey Lance, take over for me. I'm taking my break."

The second bartender nodded.

Feeling light-headed and confused, I mumbled, "Are we going to fuck now?" He placed his arms around my waist and guided me toward the backroom. In a daze, I noticed the infamous black door before me. "The Grotto," I murmured.

"Where all your fantasies come true."

"I hope so..."

He opened the door.

My eyes had to focus as the room was dark, with little light. He walked me over to a sling and undressed me. I let him, knowing he would be the first one to fuck me. Within no time, I was naked, and my prick stood at attention.

He turned me around and spread my ass cheeks. Moments later, his tongue delved deeply into my hole.

"Oh, fuck... I taste cum!"

I moaned as his long tongue entered me. The pill I swallowed made everything feel so sensual.

"You taste delicious."

His finger entered me next, and it didn't hurt, so I pressed back against it.

"You like that?" he asked.

I mumbled, "Yes."

"Careful there, buddy!" he exclaimed a few moments later as my knees gave out. He quickly caught me and guided me into the sling.

As he undressed, I couldn't help but notice the impressive sight before me. His boner was not only thick but also had an abundance of foreskin. I couldn't help but exclaim, "Your cock is huge!" This was no ordinary dick—it measured around eight inches. Damn! I thought as I realized my hand couldn't fully enclose it.

Closing my eyes, I felt the gentle pressure of his dick against my hole. In a state of deep relaxation, my body naturally welcomed him, effortlessly allowing him to enter. A fleeting thought crossed my mind. Is he wearing a condom? However, the thought quickly dissipated without further consideration.

"Oh, fuck," he moaned.

I let out a gasp of pleasure as his cock delved deeper into my ass. I lifted my head to glimpse him. He fixed his eyes on me while gripping my thighs with his hands. With each thrust, I let out a small cry, overwhelmed by the sensation. "It feels so good," I moaned. I felt consumed by the experience, repeating, "Fuck me, fuck me, fuck me," over and over. It all felt like a dream, but I knew it was real. "Fuck me!" I cried out again, lost in the moment's ecstasy.

A handsome Black man tapped the bartender on the shoulder. "Let me have a go."

The bartender withdrew and gestured for him to approach my backside. In the dimly lit room, I struggled to make out his cock, but it didn't matter. I could feel every inch as he entered me, his girth exceeding that of Brice. His tool was immense, measuring a staggering twelve inches.

"Oh, damn!" I exclaimed as he moved inside me. It didn't take long for him to gasp. "Oh, shit..." I moaned, overwhelmed by the sensation. His entire length filled me, and I felt his cum coating my insides.

"Fuck, that was hot!" Brice remarked.

The Black man pulled out.

"Oh, damn," my hole remained open, and his jizz oozed out.

Brice leaned forward and ate it.

"Fuck, yeah. Give me more."

I pushed the jizz out.

Brice moaned, "This turns me on," as he eagerly lapped every drop.

"Fuck me!" I cried out.

The bartender slid back in, filling me once again with his thick cock. He fucked me hard and fast, sending me to new heights of pleasure. I moaned as the room spun around me, and soon, we both reached our climaxes together. Brice's cock was so big that I came without touching myself, and I drifted off into ecstasy.

* * *

I woke up in a daze.

As I looked down, I saw my naked body. I tried to sit up but couldn't. I turned and noticed that I was bound to the leather sling.

"What the fuck?" My mind struggled to understand what was happening. I was dumbfounded, unable to think or say anything for a split second. Then, I remembered Brice and called out to him.

No response.

"Brice?" I shouted, louder this time.

My body began to convulse from an unknown force. I looked up and saw a man thrusting his dick inside me. Looking past him, I saw four other men watching while stroking themselves.

"Seed his ass!" one man encouraged. "The cum whore wants more!"

I realized he was referring to me. Fear gripped me as I realized this wasn't a dream. I felt raw and sensitive down below, and it hurt as he moved inside me. Turning, I saw the other men leering, eagerly awaiting their turn. Is this really happening? I thought.

"BRICE?" I yelled.

My eyes shot up in surprise, finding hands covering my mouth with tape, rendering me completely silent.

I screamed, but the sound remained trapped within the confines of my mouth. Confusion and worry filled my mind. Oh, damn... What happened to Brice? Why did he leave me?

As I gazed at the person who had just gagged me, my vision grew hazy, and I passed out.

* * *

Waking up again, I realized with horror that I was being gang-banged. The drug's influence had worn off, and I was fully conscious. I struggled against the restraints, trying to break free.

I saw a man with a black hood over his head. He was fucking me forcefully. His head shot back, and he orgasmed inside me. He pulled out, and the next man stepped forward, slapping my ass. I screamed underneath the tape.

This was not sexual—it was horrific. Tears streamed down my face as I cried out in pain. I fought against my restraints, but all I could do was bear the abuse. The men continued to line up and wait their turn. Jizz leaked from my ass, my face, and my chest.

Through tearful eyes, I screamed, "I'm done," only to be silenced by the tight grip of the electrical tape. Desperation filled my voice as I pleaded, "Listen to me!" but no words came out.

I fought back with all my might. The man fucking me came inside and pulled out, and another man stepped forward.

Everything became unfocused again, and just as I was going to pass out, I heard a familiar voice.

"He's had enough!"

With a sudden jolt, someone forcefully tore the adhesive tape away from my mouth.

I unleashed a series of desperate screams. "ENOUGH, ENOUGH, ENOUGH!" A profound disdain grew within me for the individuals surrounding me.

Hands grabbed my shoulders.

I tried to fight them off.

"It's me, Drew…"

My breath caught in my throat as I realized my friend had come and saved me. The pain from the tape's removal was intense, but I was grateful to breathe again. "Oh, Drew…" I sobbed, tears streaming down my face.

"Get the fuck out of here!" Drew spat at the onlookers, who finally realized the situation.

As Drew untied the knots, he murmured, "Everything will be fine. I'm here now…"

"Brice left me…" I murmured.

"Who?"

"The bartender." I glanced at my clothed friend, relief washing over me he didn't take part in this horrific act. "I took a pill."

"Ecstasy?"

"I… I'm not sure…"

"Stupid ass!"

The bar door creaked open, and Brice's voice reverberated from the entryway. "Hey! What's going on?" he demanded.

"Brice!" I called out.

He quickly came over to my side.

"Assist me in undoing these knots," Drew commanded.

Though puzzled by the circumstances, Brice immediately lent a hand and skillfully loosened the knots. "What on earth happened?" Brice questioned.

"I was assaulted."

"You wanted this."

"It got out of hand."

"What the hell were you thinking?" Drew snapped, confronting Brice. His eyes were blazing with fury. "You knew what was happening here, and you did nothing!"

"DREW, STOP!" I shouted.

"I had to go back to work…"

"Don't you dare… lay the blame on him!"

In the next instant, Drew's hands clenched into fists, and he circled Brice.

"STOP!" I shouted. But before I could get another word out, he lunged forward, delivering a punch to Brice's jaw.

"Are you serious?" Brice retorted.

Drew kept landing punches.

"STOP!" I yelled.

The sound of fists striking flesh reverberated around the room. Eventually, Drew stood victorious, gasping for breath as Brice lay sprawled on the floor, defeated.

* * *

I looked down into the toilet bowl, my legs wide apart, and sighed to myself. The amount of jizz that I had released caught me off guard. "I believe that's it," I commented, shaking my head in complete shock. I tried to piece together how many men had screwed me, but because of blacking out, I would never know the exact number.

As Drew flushed the toilet and aided me to my feet, Brice stepped into the bar's bathroom. He set my clothes on the sink counter and extended his hand toward me.

"Take care, buddy. I'm sorry about this."

"It's not your fault. I blame myself," I responded, looking regretful. His bruised face was a testament to the violence he had suffered, with blood seeping from his nose. "I'm sorry he hit you."

"I should press charges, but I won't."

"Thank you," I expressed gratefully.

Brice nodded and exited the bathroom.

"Piece of shit!" Drew muttered.

"Be upset with me, not him..." I said, feeling guilty about what had just happened. Drew misplaced his anger. "You shouldn't have done that."

"It's too late now," Drew replied.

I got dressed, and we left the bathroom, exiting the building. As we walked, a mix of emotions overwhelmed me—shame, guilt, and confusion. I didn't know how to proceed from this point. All I was certain of was that I needed time to process everything and figure out my next steps.

* * *

We slid into the backseat of the Uber, and as I sat there with my head forward, lost in thought, Drew leaned my head onto his shoulder. His warmth provided a sense of safety, and I felt secure enough to murmur my thanks.

"The Alexander Hotel," Drew instructed.

The driver nodded.

Once we were on our way, Drew leaned in and whispered, "I love you." Then he kissed the top of my head.

I remained silent, deep in thought.

"Johnathan?" Drew asked.

"I heard you," I replied softly.

Unease gripped me as Drew held me tightly, his intense affection suffocating my heart. The enormity of his words preoccupied my thoughts, consuming me entirely.

3

The Gloryhole

As my friend and colleague Drew filled the tub with hot water, I stood naked in the bathroom, dazed over the events of the evening.

Absentmindedly, I scratched my backside, and upon withdrawal, I felt moistness. Examining my hand, I noticed a lingering vestige of my encounter at "The Grotto"—lube and sperm.

My mind drifted to the events that had led me to this point. It all started yesterday when I arrived in Seattle for a business trip. My advertising company had invited prospective clients for a weekend of presentations, dinners, and drinks—all on the company's dime.

Having recently discovered my husband's ongoing affair, I used this trip as an opportunity for sexual exploration. The timing was right. I could no longer ignore my feelings—I needed excitement back in my life.

I snapped back to reality as my friend turned off the water. He was kneeling before me, offering care despite my reckless decisions. I didn't blame the men who had taken advantage of me. I blamed myself because I teased and made myself available to them.

Looking down, I wiped away the dried cum that caked my body. Flakes fell to the floor. I shook my head, not knowing how many men had fucked me.

Drew turned to face me, showing no judgment whatsoever.

"It's ready."

"Thank you," I murmured.

As I stepped in, Drew dipped the washcloth into the water and lathered it with soap. He washed my body, starting with my chest.

Drew's touch was comforting.

As he continued to bathe me, I studied his face. In the Uber, he confessed his love for me. At the time, I didn't respond and sat silently in the backseat, pondering his words. It was when he said my name that I answered him.

I replied, "I heard you."

I couldn't bring myself to say I love you in return. He had been a close friend for countless years, and though I found him attractive, I was committed to my marriage and firmly believed in monogamy.

I closed my eyes as his hand moved down and washed my pubes. Instantly, I became hard.

Drew didn't seem affected. He continued bathing me, and when he got to my prick, he gently pulled back the foreskin and washed the head. I was highly sensitive, and the right touch could easily set me off.

Opening my eyes, I gasped as fluid seeped from the slit. I was a huge pre-cummer. The more attention he gave me, the more fluid I produced. "I'm sorry..."

"Relax."

His touch was sensual, and I did my best to suppress my moans of pleasure. The large vein that ran down the shaft pulsed with blood. Oh, fuck... I thought if he kept this up, I'd come right away.

He washed my balls.

"Do you want me to wash your ass?"

"I'll do it," I murmured.

I elevated my rear and washed myself slowly, being extremely cautious around my hole.

"Let me have a look."

I presented my backside.

He commented, "You're not bleeding, but swollen."

"I'm not in pain," I said, turning back over.

"That's good."

As he lathered up the washcloth and started washing my legs, his mind seemed to be elsewhere.

"You know... you never responded to my comment," he stated, breaking the silence.

I knew exactly what he was referring to—our conversation in the Uber. I had been avoiding it, playing dumb, but it was time to address it. "Yes, I know I didn't..." I admitted hesitantly.

His eyes met mine, a silent question hanging between us. "Do you feel the same way?"

Drew's patience was unwavering as he waited for my response. After a deep breath, I finally voiced the truth. "I love you... but as a friend."

A sigh escaped him.

"Don't be upset," I urged.

"I'm such a fool..." he mumbled.

"No," I murmured, trying to reassure him. "If anyone's a fool, it's me. Look at what happened at 'The Grotto.' If you hadn't shown up..." My voice trailed off, guilt gnawing at my insides.

Drew dropped his gaze, a shadow of sadness crossing his face.

Would he feel better if I fucked him? The question echoed in my mind. We were the best of friends, and he was undeniably handsome. He had rescued me, and now, here I was, causing him sorrow. I owed him something.

This weekend was a no-holds-barred event. There were no rules. Anything and everything could happen, so I took the plunge and asked him. I expected him to agree to my proposition, but his reaction was quite the opposite. A grin spread across his face.

"Oh, Jonathan... you're quite amusing. You're a bottom," he reminded me.

"There's more to me than you know. I can be versatile..." This retort caused him to burst into laughter. His mirth was contagious, and I joined in, and our shared amusement echoed throughout the room. Finding humor after the incident at "The Grotto" was a welcome relief. As our glee subsided, I asked, "Would being intimate with me make you feel better?"

He nodded. "But you don't owe me anything," he gently clarified, returning to his calm demeanor.

"Ah, but I feel like I do..." I confessed.

"Oh, Johnathan..."

"I'm actually pretty good at it... you know," I explained, a hint of pride in my voice.

His chuckling resumed.

"Is that a, yes?" I inquired, hoping for a definitive answer.

His face lit up as he nodded in agreement.

Before proceeding, I wanted to ensure a mutual understanding. "We're just friends with benefits, right?"

"Yes." he agreed.

"Great!" I exclaimed.

Leaning in, I placed a gentle and innocent peck on his cheek. As I glanced back, he rose to his feet and started undressing.

Very nice, I mused internally as he revealed his seven-inch cock, rock hard and slightly bent back. Perfect for... my thoughts trailed off as desire coursed through me.

"Disappointed?" he teased.

"Far from it," I assured him, standing up, drying myself.

As I toweled off, my mind churned with thoughts. I hadn't lied when I said I loved him. He was my best friend, my confidante. There was nothing I couldn't share with him.

"I need a few minutes," he murmured.

"Of course," I agreed, wrapping the towel around my waist. I turned to him, offering a reassuring smile.

I exited the bathroom and walked toward the bar area. "Alexa... play bedroom music."

The music started playing at once.

I recognized the singer rather than the song. I grabbed a bottle of Cabernet Sauvignon off the counter, opened it, and poured two glasses. Next, I brought the wine to the bedside table, pulled back the comforter, and sat on the edge of the bed.

My dick was still hard.

I pulled back the towel and caressed myself. My cock felt good in my hand, and as the foreskin slid over the head, memories of my husband flooded my mind. He loved my foreskin, and it used to drive him crazy. I smiled at the thought, remembering how much fun our sex life had been. But then I furrowed my brow, unable to understand what had gone wrong.

Drew entered the room.

I stood up as he walked toward me, feeling a surge of anticipation. As our bodies came together, I wrapped my arms around him in an embrace. I pressed my lips gently against his, tenderly kissing him. Our tongues intertwined as a wave of desire washed over us. The kiss deepened, filled with hunger.

I moaned loudly, surprising myself.

He broke away, staring at me.

"Don't talk..." I murmured and kissed him again, not wanting to dwell on our actions. My hand then moved down to his hardness, and I caressed it. Next, I traced my fingers over his ass, which was round and firm. My digits slipped in between his cheeks and brushed against his hole, causing him to gasp.

Believe it or not, I was getting off on being the dominant one. My aggressiveness wanted to bend him over and fuck him hard, but I knew I needed to make this as sensual as possible.

I lowered him to the bed.

Leaning in, I pressed my lips against the sensitive skin of his neck, tracing a trail of kisses down to his chest. I let my mouth wander lower, paying attention to his prick, which I took into my mouth.

But it was his untouched territory that called me. I lifted his legs, revealing the most intimate part of him. I took a moment to appreciate the sight before me. Then I lowered my head, my tongue darting out to tease him.

He tensed initially, but as I continued to explore with teasing swirls, his hole relaxed, allowing me deeper access. I delved in further, my tongue probing, eliciting soft moans of pleasure from him.

My fingers replaced my tongue, slipping inside, preparing him for what was to come.

"Oh, Johnathan..."

I reached for the packet of lube and moistened his hole, then my pulsating cock. My foreskin slid back and forth over the head of my prick as I stroked myself.

"Fuck me," he moaned.

I entered, and he embraced me.

In this intimate moment, we became one, our passion intertwined. As he reached his peak, I eagerly captured his release in my mouth. The taste was divine, and I shared it with him in a tender kiss. Our connection deepened as I reached my climax. Afterward, I collapsed on the bed, breathless as I tried to calm my racing heart.

Finally relaxed, we repositioned ourselves, and I cradled his body. I kissed the back of his head and fell asleep, exhausted from the evening's events.

* * *

Waking up the following day, I turned around to spoon Drew, but he wasn't in bed. "Drew?" There was no response—he had left the room. Looking at the clock, I realized our meeting wasn't for another four hours.

Why didn't he stay in bed? I wondered, seeing a note on the bedside table.

Lifting the hotel stationery, I read, "The 'morning after' pill for gay men." My eyebrows arched in confusion. I turned and saw two white tablets.

I grabbed my phone and googled for more information. It turned out to be legit—Doxy-PEP, a new treatment that significantly reduced STD infections following unprotected sex.

He had returned to his hotel room, grabbed the pills, and brought them here for me. He knew the odds were high of me getting an STD from the ravishment at "The Grotto."

I slipped from the bed.

Reaching for the pills, I popped them in my mouth and took a sip of water from the glass he had left me.

A smile spread across my face as I reflected on our sexual encounter. I realized we were compatible, and I had thoroughly enjoyed myself.

I placed the glass down and made my way to the bathroom. Upon entering, I turned on the light and relieved myself in the toilet. My urine flowed steadily without interruption. After completely emptying my bladder, I took a shower.

As I soaped my rear end, I fingered myself. Despite the swelling, I didn't feel any pain. Taking a deep breath, I closed my eyes and contemplated "The Grotto's" backroom. I refused to portray myself as the victim. I acknowledged I had contributed to the situation and could only blame myself. "Learn from this!" I whispered. And then, unexpectedly, my cock grew rigid. I opened my eyes and gazed down, perplexed by the pleasure coursing through me.

*　*　*

I opted for a non-franchised gay coffee shop called the "Gloryhole" on Capitol Hill. Stepping inside, I settled into a corner booth and set up my laptop. A handsome barista approached the table. I placed an order for my drink and a breakfast sandwich. The server emitted a relaxed vibe, and his shoulder-length brown hair accentuated his chiseled features. He sported a band T-shirt, which complemented his faded blue jeans.

"I'll be right back with your coffee."

"Excuse me... I have a question."

He turned around. "Yes?"

"Why is this place called the 'Gloryhole?'"

"You've never been here before?"

I shook my head. "I'm here on business."

He grinned and nodded toward the back of the shop. "Check out the restroom. I'll watch your laptop."

I looked at him, questioning his response. Needing to go, however, I stood up, leaving the table.

"The first door on your left," he said.

"Thanks," I replied.

I entered the first door. The absence of urinals immediately caught my attention, clarifying that this restroom was for men who preferred privacy.

As I entered one stall, it revealed a normal-sized interior. Closing the door, a modest stainless-steel hook offered a convenient place to hang your belongings. Inside, a porcelain toilet sat against the far wall. The floor was concrete, and the walls were painted black.

Unbuttoning my jeans, I relieved myself when I heard movement in the stall beside me. Looking down, I saw the "gloryhole."

A hard, uncut cock protruded through the opening. The shaft was impressive. I saw veins tracing their way down its length, showing the intensity of its arousal. Hovering at the head, a drop of pre-cum glistened enticingly.

"Suck me."

I finished pissing.

After flushing the toilet, I kneeled and took his cock into my mouth, savoring the salty taste of pre-cum.

I deep-throated him.

The man groaned as I relished every inch, my lips gliding up and down on his shaft. His dick was of average length but had a substantial girth, making it quite a mouthful. I encircled the base with my hand and stroked him, eliciting further sounds of pleasure. I could sense his body tensing, indicating that he was nearing his climax. Quickening my pace, I sucked with greater intensity until finally, with a resounding cry, he reached his peak, filling my mouth with his warm, salty essence, which I gulped.

As he pulled away, I looked through the hole and could see the look of pure ecstasy on his face. I knew I had given him an experience to propel him through his day. I smiled, wiping away the remaining jizz on my lips.

"Thanks," he muttered.

"You're welcome."

I realized he was probably a married guy who needed to nut. What better place than a gay coffee shop? I thought.

Looking up, I saw a container attached to the wall. It held rubbers and lube packets.

I stood and removed my jeans without thinking about what I was doing. Reaching for a lube packet, I tore it open and generously applied lubricant to my hole.

Haven't you had enough? A voice inside me questioned.

As time passed, my thoughts drifted to my husband. "Fuck you," I muttered to myself, feeling a mix of anger and indifference. My newfound desire for self-gratification had overtaken my previous loyalty to him. I no longer cared about his feelings or expectations—I was determined to explore my needs.

You're addicted to sex now. As my eyes widened in contemplation at my thought, the bathroom door opened, and someone stepped into the stall beside me.

Peering through the hole, I spotted a gorgeous man. He had dark hair and olive skin, and hair covered his body. He was Mediterranean. Being direct, I whispered, "Are you interested in fucking ass?"

"Yeah."

I watched as he unbuttoned his jeans, removing a cut cock that pulsated in excitement.

"It's beautiful!" I gasped.

Standing, I presented my ass to the "gloryhole," pressing my cheeks against the wall. I hesitated momentarily, wrinkling my nose at the thought of the germs that clung to the surface. However, I quickly pushed the thought aside, reminding myself to enjoy this experience. Suddenly, I felt a finger slip inside me.

I moaned softly in response. The sensation was comforting, and I closed my eyes, fully immersing myself in the pleasure.

"You have great ass lips."

I replied, "Thanks," although in my mind, I told myself to shut up and not reveal the embarrassing truth that it was from getting fucked repeatedly.

In a deep voice, he asked, "Bareback?"

"Are you negative?"

"Yes."

"Okay."

As his five-inch prick entered me, I leaned against the nearby wall for support as he thrust inside me. This guy was good! It was so good. I came instantly, shooting on the cement floor. As he continued to pound me, I moaned in pleasure. Within seconds, his moans escalated.

"Oh, fuck..."

With one final thrust, he shot deep inside me. His groans reverberated out into the coffee shop. After he stopped spasming, he pulled out, dressed, and quickly left the stall.

"Thanks!" I muttered.

I waited for a reply, but he remained silent. Moments later, I heard him washing his hands and probably his dick, too. I stood, thinking this was unreal. I'd just swallowed a load and gotten screwed up the ass.

As I swiftly fastened my jeans, the bathroom door swung open.

"Excuse me..."

"It's all good!"

As the man who had just fucked me left, someone else entered, bumping into him.

I stood quietly.

The man walked into the stall beside me.

My curiosity got the better of me, and I peered through the hole. The man appeared to be in his late twenties. "Do you want head?" I asked.

"Yeah... But I only want the underside of my dick licked. That gets me off," he replied.

"All right."

The man unbuttoned his jeans, and his beautiful cock, which was slender but hard as a rock, appeared through the hole.

I inserted it into my mouth but then remembered his request. So, instead, I licked the underside of his glistening head.

"Oh, yes..."

I moved down his shaft and licked his clean-shaven balls. They were taunt, not saggy. When I sucked them into my mouth, it made him gasp loudly.

"Oh, fuck..."

I went back to the head of his dick and continued to lick the underside of it. Within seconds, his jizz flowed into my mouth. It was smooth, and it tasted delicious.

While he got dressed, I wiped my mouth with a tissue, ensuring there was no jizz on my face.

Coincidentally, we both exited our stalls simultaneously. He smiled and nodded his thanks, to which I responded with a smile of my own. We washed our hands and left the restroom together.

"Take care!" I whispered and made my way to my table. The young man waved in response.

The barista arrived with my sandwich and a big grin as I sat down. He must have heard the moans of passion in the bathroom.

"I need a to-go bag."

"Lost your appetite?"

I nodded in response.

"It happens a lot here." He added before returning to the counter and placing my sandwich in a box.

Opening my laptop, I pretended I hadn't just sucked off two guys and gotten fucked in the ass. The man's seed was still inside me, and I intended to leave it there.

Hearing a familiar voice, I turned to the television screen on the wall and saw Cody being interviewed by a local news reporter. I gasped excitedly.

"Can you turn up the volume?" I asked the barista while pointing toward the TV.

He nodded, increasing the sound.

"Thanks," I said gratefully.

Despite squinting, I successfully read Cody's full name at the bottom of the screen. "Cody Cromwell," I murmured. Below his name, it said City Council Member. He was being interviewed about the revitalization of the waterfront district.

I listened intently, my mind replaying our encounter at the bathhouse repeatedly. How often does he go there? I wondered.

Lost in my thoughts, I decided I'd return to "Club Emerald" after today's meeting.

* * *

I led the presentation, and it was going well. However, three-quarters of the way through, I needed to excuse myself and head to the bathroom. At that point, Drew stepped in and took over for me. After using the toilet, I left the stall and washed my hands.

The door opened.

I looked up and saw the man from Florida who had previously made a suggestive gesture toward me.

"Good presentation."

"Thanks," I said, drying my hands.

"Our company is looking for a new advertising campaign. Our budget is ten million dollars.

I glanced up, my eyes widening.

"It's between your company and our present agency." He said, giving me the universal sign for a blowjob again.

I understood him right away. If I put out, we'd get the contract.

He was cute—not attractive, but his hygiene was excellent. If I closed this deal, my bonus would be substantial. My thoughts immediately turned to exploring a beautiful, faraway destination.

"I'm uncut. Do you like that?"

He nodded.

I turned and looked at the stalls. Anyone could walk in and find us. I glanced at the door, and thankfully, it had a lock. I reached over and turned it, hearing it click in place.

Unleashing my belt buckle, I let my slacks fall to the floor. Next, I lowered my underwear, presenting my hard-on.

"Great cock!"

The man kneeled and started sucking me. He went slowly at first and then gradually quickened his pace. I would've told him to slow down, but I wanted this to end.

"If you keep that up, you'll get my load." I groaned, feeling my building eruption. "Oh, fuck…" I exclaimed moments later as a solid stream of cum shot to the back of his throat.

He moaned.

I gave him four more squirts.

After swallowing, he nodded his approval and declared, "The campaign's yours."

I smiled and pulled my slacks up. After buckling my belt, I reached into my pocket and handed him my business card. He stood, returning the favor. "I'll call you once I'm back in San Francisco."

"Sounds good."

We didn't have to say anything more. The deal was done, and I knew he was good for it. "Let me leave first," I said, in case someone was in the hallway.

"Okay. Thanks, man."

Exiting the bathroom, I returned to the event center just as Drew was wrapping up the presentation. As attendees rose to shake hands, he reminded everyone of the upcoming dinner. With that, our event would end. Everyone, including myself, would head home the following morning. However, the thought of seeing my husband did not fill me with joy.

My mind wandered to Cody.

His image lingered in my thoughts as I shook hands and thanked everyone for attending our seminar.

A tempting thought crossed my mind—what if I stayed behind? I could say I needed to wine and dine the man who had just blown me. I'd use the pretense of securing a ten-million-dollar account as justification. Surely, they would understand.

As I pondered this, Drew approached and took my hand. "We did it, buddy. It was a resounding success!" he said happily.

I let go of his hand and stared at him, wondering why he had left so suddenly this morning. He arched an eyebrow, evidently puzzled by my mood.

"What's going on?"

"Why did you take off this morning?"

"I believed it was the right thing to do," he answered.

"I wanted to hold you."

"Let's talk after dinner."

I swallowed hard, apprehensive about my next request. "I need another favor."

Drew gave me a puzzled look.

"I need to skip dinner."

Drew paused, taken aback by my statement. "You're heading back to the bathhouse?" he asked, his disappointment barely concealed.

I nodded.

He inhaled and exhaled with force.

"Fine. I'll take over... AGAIN!"

I called out his name, but he signaled that he had heard enough and walked away to greet a client with a handshake.

Composing myself, I gathered my belongings and left without saying goodbye. I knew I was wrong, but I had to find Cody.

* * *

I rushed back to the Alexander Hotel, weaving through the bustling lobby. The crowd made me wonder if extending my stay was possible. If not, no matter—another hotel would suffice. Approaching the elevator, I spotted Matteo. Just as the doors closed, I shouted, "Hold the door!" He caught my call, and his hand shot out, halting the door's closure.

As the doors reopened, I deftly sidestepped a well-dressed elderly couple. I offered Matteo my thanks, careful not to reveal our acquaintance.

"Mr. Cummings," Matteo nodded.

I couldn't help but smile, conveying my excitement at seeing him. Matteo smirked and returned his attention to the lady. "Have you been to the 'Pike Place Market' yet?"

"That's a tourist trap!" the woman snapped.

"Well, yeah... but it's a lot of fun," I interjected, my smile changing into a mischievous grin.

Matteo smirked, trying to keep his composure with the couple present. I noticed the bulge in his slacks, and he quickly covered himself.

Licking my lips slowly, I teased him. However, I understood he couldn't indulge in playfulness because of the couple. I had to respect his job.

The woman turned to me.

"Are you from here?"

"San Francisco."

"I see..." A look of disgust crossed her face. "Are you one of those 'fairies' from the Castro?" she asked, sizing me up with her eyes.

I uttered, "Excuse me?" while shaking my head, my expression revealing my complete disbelief.

With no concern for the propriety of her question, she turned her attention back to Matteo. Clearly, she belonged to the upper class and believed her status placed her above everyone else.

Her shocked husband turned and mouthed an apology to me.

I nodded while reaching into my pocket. I removed a business card and held it in my hand to give to Matteo.

As the elevator stopped on my floor, I said, "Excuse me," to the couple and extended my hand toward Matteo. I shook his hand, simultaneously slipping him my card. "Thank you for everything."

"You're welcome."

I exited the elevator and made my way to the room. Once there, I didn't waste time. I undressed and walked into the bathroom.

Looking at my reflection in the mirror, I checked myself out. I had a toned body, and my weight emphasized my physique. My soft dick was long and slender. The extra foreskin was attractive, giving it a European look.

Touching myself, I became hard right away. My girth grew to an impressive width, and the length became seven inches.

I reached under the sink for my toiletry bag and retrieved the douche hose. Entering the shower, I attached it to the handheld sprayer. Then, I applied lubricant to the hose and prepared myself for the evening.

My aim was clear—to locate Cody and clarify the misunderstanding. He had stormed out of the hotel room, under the impression that I was unfaithful to my husband.

Searching for his phone number online crossed my mind, but I quickly dismissed it, knowing it'd likely be unlisted because of his role as a City Council Member. The last thing he'd want was to be easily accessible to irate constituents.

After finishing up, I took a quick shower and dried off.

I dressed in jeans, a shirt, and sneakers, opting for simplicity. Deciding against styling my hair, I put on a ball cap. Grabbing my rain jacket, I left the room.

When I entered the elevator, I was relieved to be alone with Matteo. I stared at him and obsessed with his good looks. "I'm going to extend my stay in Seattle."

"Really?" Matteo's eyebrows perked up.

"Yes. I hope to stay here, but I might have to book another hotel."

"Si. I understand."

"Do you live nearby?"

"Capitol Hill."

I smiled—remembering it was a short walk. I wouldn't need public transportation if he invited me over. "Can I see you again?"

He smiled, reaching inside his pocket for my business card. He raised it, saying, "I'll call you!"

The elevator door opened, and two men stepped inside. I thanked Matteo with a smile.

"You're welcome."

I exited and turned back as the door closed. He was staring at me as I walked away. Sighing, I headed toward the reception desk and waited in line—thankful it moved fast.

They confirmed my suspicions—they couldn't extend my stay. They apologized, which I accepted gracefully, ensuring I understood the situation completely. It wasn't their fault, and I was confident I could secure accommodation elsewhere.

I stepped outside and booked a room at the "Pine Street Suites."

After hanging up the phone, I took a moment to collect my thoughts. It was essential to call Drew next and share my plans. I dialed the number, and he answered almost immediately.

"What's up?"

"I've decided to extend my stay," I said, barely concealing my nerves amidst his evident skepticism.

"Oh..."

"I've booked a room at the 'Pine Street Suites.' I'll call the office first thing in the morning."

"What's going on?"

"I need some alone time."

I could tell he was fishing for a deeper explanation, but I chose not to delve into details. "They won't have any issues... if you say I'm working on bringing in a new client?"

His reply was barely audible.

"Sorry, what was that?"

"Just... text me so I know you're alive."

His words struck a chord, reminding me of his intervention at "The Grotto." "I've definitely learned my lesson..."

"Have you?"

I held the phone, anticipating more, but silence followed. He ended the call.

"Fuck!"

I slipped my phone into my pocket, pushing the man's image out of my mind. I continued my walk to Capitol Hill, which offered a stunning view of Seattle. The rain had temporarily ceased, but the wind blew fiercely, causing me to wrap my jacket around me. Fall was approaching, and the dampness in the air sent shivers down my spine.

Within no time, I stood in front of the bathhouse. Before opening the door, I took a moment to contemplate deeply. With a deliberate motion, I retrieved my phone and composed a text message to Brian. "I'm prolonging my stay in Seattle. Don't call or text me." Satisfied with my message, I pressed the send button.

I opened the door.

Once again, the scent of disinfectant and eucalyptus wafted into my nostrils. The man I had encountered earlier behind the plexi-glass rose from his seat, visibly surprised by my presence. During my previous visit, he offered me his business card.

"You didn't call."

"I still have your card. I'm extending my stay..."

"Great! I hope we can get together."

"Me too!" I said, appeasing him.

After settling the entrance fee, he pushed a towel, room key, and condoms across the counter to me. Attempting to quell my nerves, I inhaled deeply and timidly inquired whether Cody Cromwell, the City Council Member, was present in the bathhouse.

With a frown, he nodded his head. "He comes here in a ball cap, head down, so no one recognizes him. He doesn't fool me, though..."

"Can I have the room next to his?"

He hesitated, recognizing my interest in him. His disappointment was apparent—he'd hoped my focus would be on him.

"Are you some kind of stalker?" He inquired, scrutinizing me closely.

I laughed softly, shaking my head. "God, no... I encountered him during my last visit. We enjoyed ourselves, but a misunderstanding led us to part ways."

He narrowed his eyes, staring at me.

"I'm not a murderer!" I exclaimed, taken aback by his probing demeanor.

"I didn't accuse you of being one," he replied, his eyes rolling as he turned to grab a different key.

I slid the old key across the counter. "I'm Johnathan, by the way."

"Andy," he responded.

"I really appreciate this."

He nodded toward the door in response.

"Thank you," I replied, relieved to leave his presence.

The lounge was humid, offering a welcome contrast to the chill outside. Undressed men with towels around their waists filled the room. As I entered, all eyes turned toward me. In response, I smiled in acknowledgment as I passed by them.

The television screen on the wall flickered with the vibrant essence of the eighties, bringing "Relax" by Frankie Goes to Hollywood to life. It was like stepping into a time capsule. The lead singer, with his undeniable charisma, stole the spotlight. His movements were provocative, moving with a rhythm that matched the pulsating beats of the song.

I continued with my routine, entering the locker room with a sense of purpose. Methodically, I stripped down, wrapping a towel securely around my waist before locking away my clothes and personal items. I skipped the showers, not needing one, and approached the exit.

In a twist of fate, as I stepped out of the locker room, I collided with the Italian gentleman I'd met on my initial night here. He immediately apologized, but his expression transformed as he looked up and recognized me. A warm, knowing smile spread across his face, greeting me like an old friend rediscovered.

"You've returned!" he voiced with delight.

"Indeed... I remember you," I responded, feeling a wave of fortune. This was the man who revealed himself to me in the lounge.

Clutching my hand, he stated, "This time, you're not getting away," and began guiding me toward a new destination.

"Where are we headed?" I asked, my interest now fully piqued.

"To my room," he answered, his grin taking on a playful edge.

I responded with a coy smile.

He guided me down a corridor, eventually ushering me into his room. Once inside, he closed the door behind us, pressing me against the wall. He then kissed me, a passionate embrace that sent waves of excitement coursing through me.

"I find you very attractive," he breathed. "I looked everywhere for you last time but couldn't find you..."

The man possessed a refined Italian accent and spoke impeccable English. His towel untied and dropped to the floor. My gaze fixated on his genitals.

There was an intriguing familiarity to it, reminiscent of someone I knew. Suddenly, Matteo's face flashed through my mind. This individual shared a similar cock.

"My name is Ciro," he said.

"Johnathan," I replied.

"Hi, Johnathan," he murmured, caressing my chest. "Do you like to get fucked?"

I nodded.

My ass had healed from the night before, but it still throbbed, not in pain, but for more cock. My prick stood rigid, thinking that this might be Matteo's brother. "Are you from Italy?" I asked.

"Yes, but I've been living in the States for a few years now," he responded, stepping back to provide a fuller explanation. "My brother and I are here to pursue our education. He's gay, just like me."

"Oh..." I gasped, realizing I was going to have sex with Matteo's brother.

Dropping my towel, he looked down, impressed with my uncut cock. I knew he was a top and wouldn't be interested in sucking me.

I kissed him.

After our embrace, he touched my head and pushed me downward.

Kneeling, I was face to face with his uncut prick. It was the same width and length as Matteo's. I pulled back the foreskin and licked the glistening head.

"Yes... Suck me..."

Even though he didn't speak Italian like his brother, his deep voice sent me into a pleasurable state.

I serviced him.

I surprised him with how well I could please him.

"That feels so good…"

I removed my mouth from his cock and licked his ball sack. After that, I ventured lower and licked the area before his hole. This sent him into gasping moans of pleasure. He smelled good. Musky and masculine, so I delved deeper and licked his opening.

"Oh, fuck, yeah… Lick my asshole."

I stopped and turned him around. I bent him over, spread his ass cheeks, and went to town. The hair around his ass was thick. His scent drove me crazy. He liked it so much that I fucked him with my tongue.

He stood me up, spun me around, and pushed me against the wall. After lubricating me, I felt his hardness invading my ass. A gasp escaped my lips as he plunged deep within. His movements mirrored the strength and steadiness of his brother. His masculinity was undeniable as he drove into me with precision.

"Fuck me!" I cried out.

"I'm coming!" He moaned moments later.

Lifting my ass, I took him deeper. I wanted his jizz deep inside, so deep it wouldn't come out. I would hold it in and use it for lubrication for Cody.

Ciro pulled out, breathless.

He fell to the bed spent.

I crawled on the bed and kissed him.

He kissed me back kindly, but I could tell his kiss lacked the sensuality of his brother's. Matteo would have kissed me deeply, melding our fluids together.

Despite this, I felt satisfied. I was content and could cross off fucking brothers from my list. It was a fantasy that I thought would never come true.

"Thank you, Ciro," I said, caressing his chest. He was hairier than Matteo and more muscular, too.

Acknowledging our encounter had ended, I eased out of bed. Securing a towel around my waist, I whispered, "I'll catch you later."

"Arrivederci!" he called out.

With a smile and a casual wave, I left the room. As I shut the door, I reminded myself mentally to keep this a secret.

I searched for Cody.

I didn't think he'd be in the open areas, so I walked the hallways. Suddenly, my nerves got the best of me. I didn't know what I'd say once I found him. "Take a deep breath. Relax," I whispered to myself.

As I passed open doors, I saw guys engaging in various sexual acts—some were getting fucked, others were giving head, and a few were getting fisted. Everything seemed to happen here.

I looked at my bungee cord and double-checked the room number. Realizing I was walking the wrong way, I turned around and headed in the opposite direction.

As I approached Cody's room, I saw the open door at the end of the hallway. It was like before—this is how I found him last time.

I wasn't sure whether to enter my room first or to peek quietly into his. Since I had nothing to put in my room, I moved forward. I took a deep breath and quietly peered around the doorframe into his room.

I caught my breath. There he was, lying on his bed, naked, with his arms behind his head.

The room was dimly lit, providing enough cover for me to sneak in and engage him intimately. It would take him a while before he realized it was me. Stop! I suppressed my thoughts. This would only make matters worse.

I cleared my throat, getting his attention.

He glanced upward and paused momentarily in disbelief that I was standing in the doorway of his room.

"What do you want?"

"Can I come in?"

He sat up and swung his legs off the side of the bed. Then he buried his head in his hands, sighing loudly. Clearly, this was too much for him.

"You left without letting me explain," I said as I entered the room uninvited. He remained seated, placing a towel over his lap.

"What you believe is mistaken... My husband is involved with another man. I uncovered this, and I'm using this weekend to reclaim the passion that's been missing from my life." I paused, anticipating his response, but he maintained his silence. "I have feelings for you... and you've stirred something deep within me."

Cody stared at me.

"I'm not lying to you."

"If what you're saying is true, why haven't you confronted him?" he asked.

"I was afraid it would end our marriage."

"It would be for the best."

Suddenly, a man entered the doorway and announced, "Sorry it took so long. I'm 'fuck ready' now!"

I turned, catching my breath.

The handsome man who entered was much younger than me. He dropped his towel, not expecting me to be in the room. His cock stood rigid. His body was slender with a small ass, the type that most guys liked to fuck.

"You found another top. Cool! A three-way," he said excitedly, noticing me.

"Oh, Jesus..." I muttered.

"Johnathan..." Cody called out.

Quickly backing up, I apologized profusely, not realizing that he had someone else joining him. "I'm so sorry for interrupting... I didn't know."

"Johnathan..." he repeated more firmly.

I turned and ran out of the room, feeling mortified and embarrassed.

* * *

Instead of hanging around and running into him later, I ran to the locker room and dressed. Andy looked up as I entered the lobby, surprised to see me leaving so soon.

"That was quick."

I nodded, notably upset. It was obvious something had happened inside. I gave him the room key and towel.

"Is everything alright?"

"No..."

I turned and left the establishment, not wanting to say anything more.

Stepping outside, I braced myself against the wind and wished I had donned a heavier coat. Pulling the hood over my head, I made my way toward Broadway, the major thoroughfare of Capitol Hill. I strolled past "The Grotto" and the "Gloryhole," both venues teeming with men. But this time, I opted not to enter. Instead, I continued searching for a different place—something dark and quiet where I could sit and soothe my restless mind.

Walking down Broadway, I stumbled upon a hole-in-the-wall restaurant named "Patrick's." Its sign advertised a lounge, perfect for my needs. I stepped inside and took a seat at the deserted bar. I'd only have to deal with the bartender with no one else around.

A dark ambiance bathed the lounge, transporting me back to the 1960s. If I lived here, I thought I'd become a regular just for its atmosphere.

The bartender noticed and approached me with a friendly smile.

"What would you like?" he asked.

"I'll have a Seagram and seven."

Nodding, he mixed the drink.

I noticed his gaze occasionally flickering toward me, trying to gauge my disposition. When he handed me the cocktail, he asked if everything was all right.

"I'll be better once I've had a few sips of this," I responded, attempting a faint smile.

He nodded understandingly and gave me space, respecting my need to unwind.

Maybe I should head home tomorrow, I wondered, suddenly realizing that my decision to extend my stay was a mistake.

A sense of detachment from the gay world consumed me. I felt like I didn't belong and couldn't grasp the inner workings and dynamics of it all.

The bartender set down another drink before me.

"This one's on the house."

His kindness prompted me to glance up and offer a smile. He was quite attractive.

He returned the smile.

"Having a tough night? Anything you want to get off your chest?"

"It's a lengthy, rather disheartening tale... I'd rather not trouble you with it."

"Understood... You're new here."

"I'm from San Francisco."

My cell phone vibrated inside my pocket. "Excuse me," I replied, retrieving it.

Matteo's name scrolled across the screen.

I picked up the call. "Matteo! Hey, what's going on?" I said, shifting my mood to a more positive one. He mentioned he had just finished work and was wondering if I'd like to meet for a drink. "I'm at..." My gaze shifted to the bartender.

He silently formed the name of the bar with his lips.

"I'm at 'Patrick's' on Broadway."

"I'll be there," came Matteo's eager reply through the phone.

"Fantastic!" I hung up and redirected my focus to the bartender. "Looking better now?"

"Yes..."

The bartender subtly adjusted his crotch.

My gaze followed the movement, and when he withdrew his hand, I noticed the unmistakable bulge straining against his slacks.

"You seem like a man who enjoys a good time," he murmured seductively.

I glanced up in surprise.

"Would you accompany me to the bathroom?" He added nonchalantly.

"I like your forwardness... What about your coworkers? What will they think?"

"This is Capitol Hill. Bathroom encounters are not uncommon. No one cares."

"Sure..."

A smirk crossed his face. "I had a feeling you were adventurous. You wanna get fucked?"

I nodded.

"I have jizz in me now. We don't need the lubrication."

"You're bad," he grinned, raising his hand to signal me to stay put—he'd be right back. I sipped my drink, disbelieving the events unfolding before me. When he returned, he had a coworker with him—an Asian guy, slender and good-looking.

"This is Justin. He'll watch the bar." Then, gesturing, he said, "Come on. Let's go..."

I looked at Justin to gauge his reaction, but he seemed indifferent. He nodded and smiled, showing that I should have a good time.

Standing up, I followed him into a single-room bathroom with a lock on the door. I knew this encounter would be quick—the faster, the better. It would distract me from thinking about Cody.

I locked the door.

We both undressed. Once I was naked, I turned around and spread my ass cheeks. He was ready and didn't require any oral stimulation. His cock was of average size, circumcised, and visibly throbbing, with the eagerness to explore the depths of my ass.

"Fuck me..." I moaned.

The bartender advanced and vigorously penetrated me. I arched back, emitting moans of pleasure.

He covered my mouth.

I enjoyed his dominant demeanor and how he took control. I loved being fucked by him.

As he breathed heavily, I knew he was approaching his climax. True to my prediction, he thrust deeply and released jets of jism, coating my insides.

"Fuck, yeah..." I exclaimed, lost in ecstasy.

He withdrew, buttoned up his slacks and shirt, and reached for the door handle. "Don't move. My buddy wants a piece of your ass."

I looked up excitedly, nodding my head.

As the door closed, I reached behind and gathered the jizz on my fingers and ate it.

A couple of minutes later, Justin walked in.

I stood with my ass cheeks spread.

He unzipped his slacks and pulled out his cock. Next, he clutched my hips and plunged his five inches inside me, continuing the bartender's fervent rhythm. He was just as forceful, and his dick head pressed against my prostate, building my orgasm. "Oh, fuck..." I cried out.

"Here it comes!" he gasped and filled me with his hot fluid at the same time.

Within seconds, I shot jets of cum onto the tile floor. Catching my breath, I turned around and licked him clean.

"Great ass, man... Thanks."

He zipped up and left.

As the door closed, I locked it.

Rising to my feet, I turned on the hot water, soaped my hands thoroughly, and washed up. After drying off with a paper towel, I slipped into my jeans and tugged my shirt over my head. Finishing up, I rinsed my mouth and looked into the mirror. As I adjusted my hair, I realized "sex" had become an obsession, and I was spiraling out of control.

4

The Brothers

After freshening up, I stepped out of the bathroom and back into the 1960s-style lounge that felt like a time capsule. As I entered, the bartender greeted me with a cocktail.

I grinned as I settled onto the barstool, catching his knowing wink—a nod to our encounter in the restroom. I chuckled and told him to thank his buddy for me as I reminisced about our encounter. Their touch still lingered, making me feel invigorated.

As the bartender left to wait on another customer, I sipped my drink, my mind drifting back to the day's events. Earlier, I had shared an intimate moment with Ciro, Matteo's brother. The memory brought a smile to my lips.

My thoughts then shifted to Cody, a man I was attracted to but was now out of my reach. I had found him at the bathhouse, only to discover a twink entering his room. I left mortified, realizing that Cody preferred younger men. It was a harsh reality, but it was time to move on. Sighing, I also remembered the men I serviced at the "Gloryhole" and, lastly, my best friend Drew back at the hotel.

Glancing at my watch, I realized Matteo was running late. He had called earlier, promising to meet for a drink. Already on my third one, I knew I needed some food to soak up the alcohol. "Is food service available?" I asked when the server returned.

"Yes, of course," he replied.

I nodded in satisfaction, spotting the perfect booth in the corner. It was secluded, offering complete privacy.

"Ciao!" a familiar voice rang out, cutting through the low hum of the lounge.

I turned, and my eyes widened in delight as Matteo walked in. He was a striking figure dressed entirely in black. Brilliantly gleaming shoes offset his jeans, button-down shirt, and leather jacket. His attire wasn't the only thing that caught my eye. His impeccably groomed hair accentuated his clean-shaven face.

"Matteo!" I exclaimed, standing to embrace him.

"Hi, Johnathan!" he responded warmly.

"Let's get a booth," I suggested, turning to pick up my cocktail glass. I signaled to the bartender that we were moving to a table.

"What's your friend drinking?" he asked.

I glanced back at Matteo, who was looking toward the lounge entrance.

"Matteo?"

"I'll take... a Negroni," he mumbled.

"What's wrong?" I asked, noting his perplexed expression as he glanced at me.

"I'm not sure..." he stammered. "This guy was staring at you when I walked in. His behavior was odd, like he was up to something."

I dismissed his concern with a casual shrug and pointed toward our chosen booth. "I'm sure it was nothing." Glancing back at the bartender, I ensured he had heard Matteo's drink order.

He nodded. "One Negroni, coming up."

Upon reaching the booth, we paused momentarily, deciding where to sit. "Should we sit across from each other or side by side?" I queried.

"Together," he murmured, a smile playing on his lips.

As we settled into the booth, a wave of anticipation washed over me. When I looked at Matteo, he met my gaze with a warm smile. I leaned in to share a kiss, feeling an electric current surging through me. His Italian cologne filled my senses, making the moment even more intoxicating.

My hand reached his thigh, which was firm and muscular under my touch. Our moment abruptly stopped when Matteo pulled away, glancing up at the bartender. I hadn't realized he was standing at our table.

The bartender had a boner.

Matteo snickered.

The server placed the menus and the drink on our table, his eyes lingering a bit too long.

"I'm sorry for interrupting. I'll return for your orders," he said, retreating with a noticeably seductive grin.

"He's quite the flirt," Matteo observed, causing us to giggle.

Regaining my composure, I asked, "Now that we're alone," I began, my voice dropping to a whisper, "tell me everything about yourself."

He smirked at my request, clearly enjoying the attention. Our time together was just beginning, and I looked forward to learning more about him.

"I'm from Taormina, a beautiful city in Sicily. You might be familiar with it?" he asked.

I nodded in acknowledgment.

"I'm pursuing a degree in Hospitality Management."

"Are you staying here after school?"

He shook his head. "My brother and I will return home and manage our family's hotel."

Seeing my opportunity, I asked, "Your brother? He's here with you?"

Matteo nodded. "Si, he's in school, too!"

"What's his name?" I queried.

"Ciro."

A smile spread across my face. First, to acknowledge Matteo's statement and second, to confirm my suspicion—I had sex with his brother. Everything clicked into place. They were here to gain an education, relish their youth in a foreign country, and then return home.

"May I visit you in Italy?" I asked.

"Of course..." he affirmed with a warm smile.

The thought of vacationing there brought a smile to my face. The prospect of indulging in late-night dinners and romantic strolls through his hometown was enticing.

The bartender's return momentarily interrupted our conversation. We glanced at the menu, and I decided on the grilled chicken breast with vegetables while Matteo went for the Chicken Marsala. As we savored our meals, we kept up the light and enjoyable conversation. Once we finished, I paid the bill, left a generous tip, and expressed my gratitude to the server.

"I hope you come again?" the bartender hinted, a playful smirk on his face.

"He's friendly," Matteo chuckled in response.

"Yes, he is," I replied, sharing his amusement.

With our evening still young, we left the lounge and walked down Broadway Avenue, peering into the shops as we continued our conversation. I opened up about my marriage and my husband's infidelity.

"I'm sorry," Matteo said sincerely.

"Don't be," I replied, a smile tugging at the corners of my lips. "Meeting you has made me extremely happy."

Before long, we strolled through Volunteer Park, home to the "Conservatory" and the "Asian Art Museum." Despite the darkness, we felt safe in the tree-covered park. As our walk continued, we realized we weren't alone. After dark, this place transformed into a haven for men who engaged in sexual acts. We passed men getting fucked, sucked, and gang-banged as we made our way through the darkness.

The chilly weather prompted us to pause at one point, and Matteo pulled me into his arms.

"You make me feel good," he muttered.

"I like you too," I confessed.

"Watching these men has excited me."

His deep voice was undeniably romantic.

"My apartment's nearby," he suggested, his eyes gleaming with anticipation. "Ho bisogno di venire," he whispered, his voice trembling with desire.

"I don't understand," I admitted.

"I need to cum," he clarified, guiding my hand to his throbbing erection.

"Let's go…" I breathed out.

His apartment was only a block away. As we approached, the multi-story building stood tall and imposing under the soft glow of the streetlights. The tan brick facade bore age marks, giving it an old-world charm. "It's beautiful," I remarked, taking in the structure.

Matteo pushed open the heavy front door, revealing the interior. "Welcome to my home," he announced.

I gasped at the sight of the grand staircase that greeted us. Its intricate spiral design and detailed craftsmanship were nothing short of impressive. The polished wooden handrails gleamed under the light, and the floor tiles added style, evoking memories of a bygone era.

"We're on the top floor," Matteo informed me, leading the way.

My mind wandered back to Ciro. I recalled our encounter at the bathhouse—a fleeting yet intense moment that had left a lasting impression. His brother's raw masculinity had stirred something within me.

We stepped into the elevator, its antiquated design a testament to the building's history. Matteo closed the metal gate before operating the lift. As we ascended, the engine's hum filled the air, accompanied by the distinctive smell of mechanical grease.

Upon reaching the top floor, we exited the lift and walked down a long hallway. Matteo's apartment was at the end, marked by a beautifully crafted door adorned with an elegant brass knocker.

Matteo inserted his key into the lock and turned it. With a soft click, the door swung open.

As I entered, the apartment welcomed me with its cozy furnishings, emanating a warm and inviting atmosphere. I removed my jacket at Matteo's suggestion and settled onto the couch.

A few moments later, Ciro came out of the bathroom, completely naked. His toned body was damp from the shower, and his olive skin glistened in the room's soft light.

As he stood, I noticed the substantial size of his flaccid cock, which hung between his legs. I found myself unable to look away.

"We have a guest," exclaimed Matteo.

Ciro's eyes widened upon recognizing me.

"Hi!" he responded.

My breath hitched in my throat as he stepped forward. Most people would have excused themselves and gotten dressed, but not him—he extended his hand for a shake.

"Ciro..." he murmured. His eyebrow arched, questioning how I intended to address him.

"I'm Jonathan. It's a pleasure to meet you…"

Upon realizing I would be evasive, he gave a knowing smirk, clearly amused by my unease. This had now turned into a game, and he was ready to revel in it.

I couldn't believe he was standing naked before me. I glanced down and saw his growing erection. The natural beauty of his cock left me in awe. The prominent vein running down the shaft pulsed with life, and in no time, his prick stood erect, throbbing with anticipation.

"I hope I haven't made your guest uncomfortable," Ciro commented, glancing at his brother. "Does he know we're nudists?" he added, smirking.

"He does now…" Matteo responded, grinning as he subtly adjusted the noticeable bulge in his jeans.

"My brother has excellent taste in men. You're incredibly handsome, Johnathan. Look at what you've done…" He gestured toward his boner.

"Thank… you?" I stammered out, taken aback.

I glanced at Matteo for some guidance, only to find him grinning at his brother's antics, apparently unperturbed.

"I'll be back in a moment," Ciro declared, flashing a cheeky wink.

As he turned and walked away, his departing figure immediately captivated my attention. His ass was taut and sculpted. The enticing cleft between them was pronounced, guiding my eyes to his thighs.

"You were staring at his dick," Matteo muttered.

I shook my head, struggling to comprehend the situation. "Well, yeah… It was right there in front of me," I retorted. "Was there a hint of jealousy in his tone?" To ease his mind, I confessed I found his dick more appealing than his brother's.

"Oh, no, no… You misunderstood," he quickly responded, waving his hands. "We're brothers… There's no competition," he explained, his thick Italian accent coloring his words. "My English... Not so good. I wanted to know if you liked what you saw?"

"Are you upset with me?" I asked, seeking clarification before answering his question.

"Certainly not."

"I found it quite intriguing."

"Do you want to play with it?" he offered.

His boldness took me aback. I paused for a moment to contemplate his proposal. I couldn't believe I was being offered the opportunity to engage in such an activity. "His prick is identical to yours," I clarified.

"Like mine? I don't understand."

"Your dicks are the same."

"Oh..." he laughed. "I see. Maybe that's why I enjoy playing with it so much."

After a few seconds of silence, I laughed, assuming he was joking. However, I realized he was serious when he didn't join in. Suddenly, a surge of excitement coursed through me. I reached forward and caressed myself. "If what you said is true, that turns me on," I admitted.

Matteo nodded. "It's true."

"Are you looking for a threesome?" I asked.

He nodded again.

"And will Ciro be interested?"

Matteo, with a roll of his eyes and a grin, replied, "My brother is horny. Yes, he'll be interested."

"All right."

"Now... what can I get you to drink?" he queried, smoothly shifting the conversation.

"I'll take a beer."

His dark brown eyes captivated me as he leaned forward and gently traced his fingers along my chin. His presence instilled a sense of calm within me. I was convinced he felt the same way because he shared his secret relationship with his brother.

Flashing a smile, he playfully put his finger inside my mouth. Then he withdrew it and promised to return with our beverages.

"You're a tease..." I murmured.

I watched as he left the room, excited about the situation but apprehensive about whether Ciro would reveal our acquaintance. Suddenly, pre-cum oozed from the head of my dick, distracting my anxious thoughts. I caressed myself again, thinking I might have sex with brothers. These two seemed entirely comfortable with each other. Was this a cultural thing in Italy? I hoped so.

Tell him the truth. I thought.

Adjusting my boner, I allowed it to extend to its full length. I caressed myself again. When I removed my hand, I noticed the damp spot on my jeans.

Within minutes, Matteo returned, carrying two Italian beers. His cock was still hard and pulsating through his jeans. I could see the wet spot forming at the tip of his dick. He was a heavy pre-cummer, too.

I patted the couch next to me. "Please sit. I have something to tell you."

Matteo hesitated, looking bewildered. He set the drinks down. "Have I made you uncomfortable?"

"No," I reassured him.

Looking relieved, Matteo sat down.

"I know Ciro."

He paused. His eyebrows furrowed. "You know my brother? How's that possible? You don't live here."

"I met him at the bathhouse."

Matteo pondered deeply. "Oh..." he exclaimed in understanding moments later.

"We had sex."

Matteo leaned back and seemed to think again. After a couple of seconds, he asked, "Did he fuck you?"

I nodded.

"This does not bother me..."

A door swung open abruptly, causing Matteo and me to turn toward the interruption. I didn't have time to dwell on his response. It was Ciro, now dressed in jeans and a T-shirt, confidently striding into the room. Ignoring our surprised glances, he headed straight for Matteo's beer. Without asking, he picked up the bottle and took a satisfying swig. The amber liquid disappeared down his throat, and he released a contented sigh before replacing the bottle on the table.

Afterward, he sauntered over to me, his eyes twinkling with mischief. Flashing a charming smile, he plopped down beside me.

With both men at my sides, a wave of anxiety washed over me. Their overwhelming presence was suffocating, making it difficult to breathe.

"Ciro?" I stuttered, wanting to clarify the situation.

"Si?"

"I told Matteo we had sex."

"I'm glad because if you hadn't, I would've. I don't keep secrets from my little brother."

Pivoting toward Matteo, I sought his response. In return, he offered a nod of agreement, seamlessly blending into the momentum of the situation.

My eyes followed Matteo as he turned his gaze toward his brother, studying the features that mirrored his own. I sat silently, watching a smile form on his lips, acknowledging their silent conversation. Moments later, Matteo nodded affirmatively.

Ciro grinned, returning the nod.

Within seconds, Matteo leaned forward and removed his brother's shirt. Ciro immediately caressed his pecks, displaying his muscles for me.

I stared in surprise.

They both seemed to derive pleasure from knowing I was watching them. Ciro sighed moments later, flicking his erect nipples.

"Look how hard they are," he said, pinching the hardened nubs. "Let's show Johnathan how much fun we have together," he murmured, glancing at his brother.

Matteo responded with an eager grin.

Gently, Ciro guided Matteo's head toward one of his nipples. "Is this making you uneasy?" He queried softly, his fingers lightly brushing the back of Matteo's head.

I responded with a shake of my head as the sound of suction filled the air.

Matteo then drew back from Ciro's chest, his lips seeking mine in a fervent kiss. It was a startling and electrifying moment, taking me by surprise.

I pulled away momentarily to remove my shirt. Once shirtless, Ciro's hands roamed my chest, eager to explore my masculine body.

With an air of confidence and nonchalance, I watched as Matteo stood and shed his shirt, jeans, and underwear, baring his naked form. His raw masculinity took my breath away.

Ciro stood up, wrapping his arms around his brother's torso. An intense moment of eye contact passed between them. Then, his fingers began a slow exploration, tracing the contours of Matteo's chest and then his firm abdomen.

The playful interaction stirred something deep within me. I held my breath as Ciro's hand ventured lower, nearing Matteo's hardness, only to halt abruptly.

"Do you want me to grab his dick?"

His question hung in the air, heavy with anticipation.

I nodded.

He smirked teasingly. Instead of grabbing Matteo's cock, he leaned in and kissed him sensually on the lips. It started as a peck, and then their tongues intertwined passionately.

I could sense their deliberate intention to excite me. They understood this was a fantasy becoming a reality, and they skillfully played their roles to the fullest.

"I don't suck cock," he murmured, "but my brother does it very well." Within no time, he shed his jeans and underwear, revealing his hard-on. All seven inches of it pulsated with excitement. Pre-cum oozed from the tip as he stood naked before us. I wanted to reach for it but remained motionless, awaiting direction.

"Taste my pre-cum!"

Ciro pushed Matteo's head down. I watched as Matteo took his brother's cock in his mouth. He swallowed all seven inches, deep-throating him.

I watched, dumbfounded.

Matteo pulled back, grabbing Ciro's ass playfully. "We're very close... I pleasure him regularly."

"Okay..." I uttered in disbelief.

Ciro draped his arm around Matteo's shoulder, drawing him closer. "My little brother, you don't need to reveal our secrets to Johnathan," he said. He tousled Matteo's hair and smiled, turning back to me. "He already understands our relationship."

"This is my first with brothers," I confessed.

"We'll be gentle with you," Matteo promised, his eyes brimming with love and tenderness.

A few seconds later, Ciro's intense glare in his eyes startled me. "He's a man, Goddamnit!" Ciro's voice rose, his hands gesturing emphatically in characteristic Italian fashion. "Treat him as one."

"I'm fine, Matteo. You're very sweet..."

Ciro gestured for me to stand. "Enough of this girlish talk. It's time to have fun..."

For a split second, I saw Ciro's temperament. I let it go, not wanting to ruin the moment. I stood and shed my jeans. My dick sprung forward, freed from the confines of my designer underwear.

Ciro ran his hand over my length.

I moaned as he touched me.

Next, he drew us all together, his gaze intense and alluring. He held Matteo and me close, his hand firm on our backside. His lips met mine in an electrifying kiss, igniting a fire within me.

Shortly after, I felt another set of lips on mine.

Matteo's kiss was softer but more passionate. I was caught in this intoxicating dance, going back and forth between them.

And then, at one point, Ciro pulled Matteo closer. He paused, looking into his brother's eyes.

"I'm sorry for raising my voice."

Then, he gently kissed Matteo's forehead, a tender gesture that belied the moment's intensity. The energy shifted then, becoming more intimate.

Matteo nodded, accepting his apology.

Ciro kissed his brother once more on the lips. As he pulled away, Matteo drew him back and passionately kissed him. After a few moments, Ciro turned toward me, smiling happily.

The kiss from his brother stirred something within him. His arousal was evident as a large amount of pre-cum dripped onto the hardwood floor.

He pushed me to my knees.

As I opened my mouth, they stepped forward, their boners ready for servicing. With my hands at the base of their cocks, I guided their heads into my mouth, feeling the velvety texture of their foreskin against my tongue. The pre-cum that coated their pricks had a salty tang. I shut my eyes, relishing the moment. The sensation of having two cocks in my mouth was overwhelming. I moaned softly, lost in the pleasure that these two men were giving upon me.

Their identical cocks filled my mouth, and I found it challenging to accommodate them. As I tried to adjust, I choked. It seemed to turn Ciro on because he grabbed my head and pushed deeper into my throat.

With tears forming in my eyes, I struggled to breathe. The sensation was intense, and it added to the thrill of the experience.

With a firm grip on my hair, Ciro yanked my head back, forcing me to look upwards.

"Suck my brother!" he commanded.

Obediently, I leaned forward to take Matteo's exquisite cock into my mouth. I relished every inch of him, causing him to emit a moan of pure delight. His anticipation dripped from the tip, sparking excitement within me.

"This feels incredible," he gasped.

I continued to suck him, then moved lower to lick his balls and taint. After a few moments, he gently pulled away.

"Now it's my brother's turn," he said.

Turning to Ciro, I found him stroking his cock, evidently aroused by watching me service his brother.

"Put your tongue inside my foreskin," Ciro instructed in his thick Italian accent.

His deep voice sent chills down my spine. Eagerly complying, I slipped my tongue into the opening, eliciting a moan from him.

"He likes it!" Ciro chuckled.

Watching Matteo stroking himself excited him further. A broad grin spread across his face as he spoke Italian to his brother.

"Let's fuck him together!" he proposed.

Matteo nodded in agreement.

I didn't understand their conversation, but it didn't matter. I was too caught up in the moment's pleasure.

Without warning, Ciro withdrew from my mouth and claimed a spot on the couch. He lifted his legs and spread his cheeks, presenting himself to me.

"Lick my asshole," he ordered.

I dropped to my knees and extended my tongue, initially circling his entrance. I pulled away momentarily to clear the thick hair obstructing my path. Returning to my task, I tongued him again, unhindered this time. As he relaxed, I ventured deeper with my tongue, essentially pleasuring him with it.

He let out a moan and grasped the back of my head, encouraging me to delve even deeper. His musky scent sent waves of desire coursing through me.

As I licked Ciro's ass, Matteo reached down and stroked my cock. I pulled away from Ciro and cautioned him, "I'm highly sensitive..."

"Si. Si..."

Matteo inserted his finger inside my ass. It didn't require any lubrication because of my earlier sexual escapade.

Meanwhile, I continued to tongue Ciro's ass. Shortly after, I heard the coffee table shifting, followed by Matteo's dick pressing against my fuck hole.

As he entered, his shaft stretched me, causing a painful sensation at first. I relaxed my muscles and instructed him to go slowly.

Matteo paused momentarily, allowing me to acclimate to him before pushing himself further inside. I could feel every ridge of his cock as he slid deeper. It was a sensation unlike any other, and I moaned as he moved back and forth.

The sound of flesh slapping against flesh filled the room as his hips picked up speed. I could feel my dick growing harder and harder with each thrust, and I knew I was going to come soon.

I stroked my prick as I ate out Ciro's ass.

Matteo was relentless, and he continued to pound me. Moments later, my head tilted back in ecstasy as I released, splattering jizz onto the hardwood floor.

Matteo filled me with his hot fluid.

"Your ass is so moist and warm," he exclaimed, out of breath. "I love fucking you..."

I kissed Matteo, thanking him.

"My pleasure..."

Ciro lowered his legs.

"It's my turn. Sit on my cock," he demanded, playing the role of the aggressor.

I watched him lie back and stroke eagerly, waiting for my ass. "I love sloppy seconds."

I glanced at Matteo.

He gestured forward. "Give my brother what he wants..."

Not wasting any time, I crawled on top of Ciro and faced him. As I turned to grasp his cock, he halted me.

"I want Matteo to insert it," he declared.

I turned back around and engaged him in a passionate French kiss. Moments later, I felt Matteo's head at my ass. Turning, I watched him deep-throating his brother. After a few seconds of delivering sloppy head, he guided Ciro's cock inside me.

I gasped initially at the intrusion, then began moving up and down, savoring every inch of his firmness. I was so well-lubricated that his prick moved back and forth effortlessly within me.

"That's right... Enjoy his cock!" Matteo moaned.

Ciro gripped my waist and aided my movements, enjoying being the dominant one. "You like fucking brothers, don't you?" he teased.

I moaned in ecstasy.

"I knew you were kinky." He grinned, slapping my ass hard enough to leave a welt.

"Fuck me!" I moaned.

I turned back to Matteo in ecstasy, noticing he was stroking his boner. His arousal never waned.

"Put your dick in his ass," Ciro directed.

I looked back at him, my eyes widening in surprise. "Double penetration?" I muttered, never experiencing it before. "I don't know..."

Ciro hushed my worries. "You can do this..." His voice was soothing despite the carnal desire that shone in his eyes. He wanted me to take both of them at once.

As Ciro continued to guide me up and down, he moaned in ecstasy. "You feel amazing. I can feel my brother's jizz in your ass. It's so warm..." he said, clearly turned on by the sensation.

"I want you, Matteo." I cried out, turning toward him, consumed with desire.

"Spread your cheeks," he instructed.

I halted my movements and followed his orders.

I felt the tip of his dick against my hole. At first, it didn't penetrate, and the pressure was uncomfortable. But as I relaxed, his cock slid right in, and I was now accommodating two engorged pricks.

They took turns pleasuring me, alternating their movements. I continued kissing Ciro deeply until he started moaning loudly, signaling his impending release. His climax filled me. The sensations were overwhelming.

Matteo's cock took over, thrusting back and forth inside me. His stamina was truly remarkable. He shot his second load deep within me, and I gasped as their combined jizz seeped from my ass. With both cocks still inside me, I pleasured myself to ejaculation.

Ciro guided my head to his chest.

"Eat your cum!" he demanded.

As their cocks slipped from me, I cleaned the remnants from his chest, savoring every drop in my mouth before swallowing it.

"It's time to shower," Ciro announced, giving my backside another slap.

I rose to my feet, taken aback by his sudden change in demeanor. I observed him exchanging glances with his brother before he silently strode toward the bathroom.

Matteo took my hand, and we followed Ciro. Once inside the bathroom, Matteo embraced me tenderly. He was kind, expressing appreciation of my willingness to please them.

"Thank you," he murmured.

Ciro stepped into the shower.

"Is he all right?" I whispered, concerned that he had ended things unexpectedly.

"He feels guilty afterward..."

"Oh..."

While Ciro bathed, Matteo continued to shower me with kisses. He had a gentle soul, and I was worried about him. "How are you?" I asked.

Matteo shifted uncomfortably, his gaze dropping to the floor. He seemed to wrestle with an internal struggle before finally meeting my eyes again.

"Sometimes," he started, his voice barely above a whisper, "I wish my brother would do more..."

He trailed off, his sentence hanging in the air unfinished. The silence was deafening. I reached out, grasping his hand. He didn't have to voice it out—I could see it clear as day. Matteo yearned for a deeper connection with his brother. I couldn't fully comprehend it, but it wasn't for me to question.

"I understand," I whispered.

"Thank you."

Moments later, Ciro stepped out of the shower and dried himself with a towel.

"Okay, lovebirds... It's time to get cleaned up."

His disposition seemed to have changed for the better. We broke apart and stepped into the shower. As Matteo bathed me, he became aroused again.

"Voglio fare l'amore con te."

I didn't need further clarification. Turning my ass toward him, I whispered how much I desired him.

* * *

As I stepped out of the apartment building, a warmth radiated within me, undisturbed by the biting chill outside. I had wanted to stay the night, but Matteo insisted he needed some alone time with Ciro. "This was always the case after our threesomes," he explained. I kissed him goodbye, hoping our paths would cross again.

As I walked down the street, my mind drifted to my marriage. Was it over? Could I forgive Brian for his infidelity? Unresolved questions besieged me, and I was unsure what action to take. However, as I continued walking, lost in thought, I realized that time was on my side. The answer would eventually reveal itself.

I heard someone behind me. Squinting, I turned around, struggling to make out the stranger's silhouette. When he realized I had seen him, he turned and walked in the opposite direction.

The man's height and profile seemed familiar, but I didn't recognize him. I picked up the pace, thinking it was odd. I didn't feel scared because I only had a few blocks left until I reached the business district.

Turning back around, I saw the stranger again. His dark silhouette advanced toward me. My heart fluttered, thinking this wasn't happening. I took off running, beating him to safety.

As I stopped and turned around, the stranger also halted, staring at me momentarily before running away.

"What the hell?" I whispered, struggling to catch my breath.

Spinning back around, I made my way toward the hotel. I passed the lively bars, content with my evening. I required no more stimulation. Glancing over my shoulder, I confirmed the stranger was no longer there. He had vanished, no longer tailing me.

Descending the hill, I walked past the bathhouse. I wondered if Cody might be there. A sigh escaped me, and I felt sad as I thought about our fizzled connection. He was a good guy, and I genuinely liked him. As I passed a group of young men, their excitement was evident as they headed for a night out. I couldn't help but smile at their naivety. It brought back memories of when I was their age.

"Johnathan?"

I turned around, spotting the silhouette of someone approaching me. I wasn't sure whether to stop or start running for a moment.

"It's me, Andy?"

I halted as he stepped forward. As his face came into view, I recognized his smile.

"Andy, from the bathhouse?"

"Oh, hi!" I remembered him now. He was the guy behind the plexiglass at the check-in counter. "What a surprise! Did you just get off work?"

"I've been off for a while. Just out for a stroll..."

"Nice," I responded, feeling a tad uncomfortable. I wanted to keep walking but didn't want to appear rude.

"So, what are you up to?" he asked.

"I'm heading back to my hotel."

"Would you like to come over? Have a beer? We could watch a movie or just hang out."

His request caught me off guard. "I'll pass. It was good seeing you, though."

"Yeah... Have a good evening."

His disappointment was obvious. I waved, turned around, and resumed my walk. I knew I had been rather abrupt, but I was genuinely exhausted. Glancing over my shoulder, I saw him heading in the opposite direction. With a nonchalant shrug, I refocused and resumed my stride.

Entering the Alexander Hotel, I bypassed the reception desk and headed for the elevator. The night shift operator was working. He was an older gentleman, and I found him professional. I acknowledged him with a nod and informed him of my floor.

As the door opened, the operator gestured for me to exit. "Enjoy your evening," he said.

I nodded and stepped out, making my way to my room. Once I reached it, I unlocked the door and entered, relieved to be there.

Stepping inside, I shed my clothes and slipped into my jogging pants and T-shirt, craving comfort. Afterward, I opened the small refrigerator to inspect its contents. In need of something refreshing, I grabbed a Diet Coke. Forgoing a glass, I opted to drink it straight from the can.

A knock at the door interrupted my sipping. I walked over and peered through the peephole. It was Drew. I swung the door open.

"Hi!"

"Can I come in?"

"Of course," I said, stepping aside. He stepped through the doorway and turned to face me. His cheeks were flushed as if he had been outside running a marathon.

"Are you extending your stay?" he asked.

"I think so..." I responded.

"Can we talk?"

"Sure." My forehead creased in confusion.

"I'm insanely jealous of Cody."

"Oh, Drew... I saw him at the bathhouse. He's moved on... and so have I." I stared at him, unable to grasp his emotional distress. Recognizing this, I regretted my decision to sleep with him. I had only added fuel to the fire.

A grin gradually spread across his face, and he seemed pleased with my response. Without warning, he moved closer, pressing his lips against mine. What began as a peck quickly turned into a passionate kiss.

I pulled away, surprised.

"Jonathan?" he inquired.

"I wasn't expecting that," I confessed.

"I want to make love to you," he declared, his eyes ablaze with desire.

"We need to talk," I interjected, determined to keep this from spiraling out of control and jeopardizing our friendship.

His brow furrowed in confusion.

"Would you like something to drink?" I asked, motioning toward the mini-fridge.

"A Coke would be fine."

As Drew settled onto the couch, I grabbed his beverage and joined him. "Drew," I began, taking a deep breath before continuing, "I'm married."

"And?" he prodded.

"I love Brian."

"YOU'RE FORGIVING HIM?"

"I don't know... I might. After this weekend, he'll have to forgive... me!" I said, thumping my chest.

Drew exhaled loudly, clearly frustrated.

"We're supposed to be fuck buddies," I said.

"We are!" he retorted.

"You're acting like an obsessed lover," I countered.

Drew sat motionless, absorbing my words.

"I've been with multiple guys tonight." I handed him his drink, trying to tally the number of encounters in my head but failing.

"I'm well aware!" he spat.

"How could you possibly know that?"

"Of course you have. You went to the bathhouse," he corrected, avoiding my gaze.

"As absurd as it may sound, I needed to... embrace my inner slut..."

Drew's attention immediately focused back on me. "BRIAN'S A JERK! HE DESERVES THIS!"

His outburst left me stunned.

Taking a moment to sip my Coke, I shared the rest of my evening. "After leaving the bathhouse, I ended up with the bartender at "Patrick's" and his co-worker."

"Yeah."

His nonchalant response took me aback. It was as if he already knew about my encounter. "Then, I had sex with Matteo, the hotel's lift operator, and his brother."

"His brother?" he echoed in shock.

As I replayed the evening's events, I realized the extent of my actions. It was extreme. I wasn't proud of what I had done, but I felt compelled to tell him everything. He needed to understand we were better off as friends.

"I see what you're doing." With his gaze locked onto mine, Drew declared, "I will never hate or despise you. I don't like you having sex with other men." He paused for a breath. "But I understand. Let me fuck you..."

His words left me speechless. It felt as though he was staking his claim. My eyes narrowed as I observed his pleading expression.

"Drew, no..."

"No?"

Suddenly, Drew turned aggressive and pinned me to the couch. Just as I was about to yell and demand that he stop, he kissed me. I tried to turn my head, but he held me securely in place. As his tongue invaded my mouth, I surrendered.

"I want to rim you."

I quickly calculated the number of men I'd been with once again. This time, a number came to mind. It was probably inaccurate, but I threw it out there anyway. "I've been with six or seven guys. Maybe more..." This was my last-ditch effort to snap him out of his delusional mindset.

"I DON'T CARE!" he declared emphatically, proceeding to undress me. After tossing my jogging pants and underwear onto the floor, he hoisted my legs into the air.

"Give me the cum in your ass."

"No..."

"DO IT!" he demanded.

I parted my ass cheeks.

"Push it out!"

Taking a deep breath, I depressed my abdomen, and within seconds, the jizz trickled out.

"Fuck yeah..." Drew murmured.

He kneeled, adjusting my legs for better access, and pleasured me with his mouth. He voraciously swallowed the cum as it flowed out of me.

When there was no more left for him to feast on, Drew stood and discarded his jeans. His erect dick sprang forward, pulsating like a snake ready to strike. I removed my shirt and repositioned myself on the couch, raising my legs higher in preparation.

He bent over and penetrated me.

My head arched back as I felt the sensation of his cock brushing against my prostate with each thrust. His movements were swift and rhythmic—it was an intoxicating blend of pleasure and pain.

"Oh, God..." I moaned in ecstasy.

He was an exceptional lover, and I yearned for his mouth on mine.

"Kiss me..." I requested softly.

He complied, leaning in to share a passionate kiss while maintaining the rhythm of his thrusts. The distinctive curve of his dick sent waves of pleasure through me.

"You could have me every night."

"I want you..." I responded, lost in the throes of passion.

He pulled away and then instructed me to turn over. Without a moment's hesitation, I did as he asked.

He pushed my head down onto the couch, holding it in place as he continued his movements. He was determined to keep his pace until he gifted me with cum.

"Here it comes," he groaned.

"Yes..." I breathed out, my heart pounding.

"DO YOU WANT IT?" he shouted.

"CUM IN ME!" I responded, matching his intensity.

With one final, powerful thrust, he filled me with his hot fluid. My eyes rolled back in ecstasy as I felt the rush of his release within me.

As he continued to thrust, driving his jizz deeper inside me, I knew it wouldn't be leaving anytime soon. As I caught my breath, a loud knock at the door interrupted us.

Drew withdrew from me.

Turning, I slid to the floor. I thought perhaps we'd been too loud. I saw Drew's prick still pulsating, his cum dripping onto the carpet. "It must be hotel security."

I stood and gestured for him to dress.

"Hold on... I'll be right there," I called out, hurriedly pulling on my jogging pants. I approached the door and swung it open. To my surprise, Cody was standing there. His presence took me aback.

"Can I come in?" he inquired.

"I'm not alone," I responded, glancing at Drew, his face suddenly pale. "This really isn't the best moment..." I started, but Cody brushed past me before I could finish. I gasped as I understood stopping him wasn't an option.

Cody sniffed the sex-laden air. My state of partial undress was also an unmistakable testament to our recent activity.

"So, I'm intruding... on your intimate moment?" he deduced.

I glanced at Drew as he buttoned up his jeans, making denial impossible. So, instead of attempting to lie, I shrugged, surrendering.

Cody turned toward Drew and extended his hand.

"I'm Cody Cromwell."

Drew, however, remained motionless, a sneer etched into his face.

"Okay?" Cody questioned, raising his eyebrow in confusion.

As Cody shifted his attention back to me, I shot Drew a warning look, silently urging him to behave.

"You left the bathhouse."

"That twink was there!"

Drew crossed his arms over his chest, knowing he wasn't part of the conversation. I turned toward him and mouthed, "I'm sorry," before pivoting back to Cody. "This isn't a good time. You should leave..."

"I'm not leaving until you hear what I have to say... I'm sorry for not listening to you. I realize my mistake and regret it immensely."

My breath caught in my throat. His words were the validation I had been yearning for. As he stepped forward to embrace me, I backed up, glancing at Drew. He seemed disoriented, his face flushing as he watched the situation unfold. Suddenly, he snatched the can of Coke and started for the door.

"Drew, don't leave..." I pleaded.

His lips, usually curved into a captivating grin, were now downturned in a subtle frown, revealing his deep-seated disappointment and anguish.

"Drew..."

"I know my place." With those words, he swung the door open and exited the room.

"What's going on?" Cody inquired as the door closed, noticing my stillness.

"He's my friend," I responded.

"You're having sex with your best friend?"

I gestured to show that I would not discuss it. I felt awful. Drew was my friend, and I had been treating him horribly. "It's a long story," I murmured, breathing deeply. "Explain to me why you're here again."

"I came to apologize," he responded.

I crossed my arms. "So... did you enjoy the twink? Was he everything you hoped for? Did he have a tight ass?"

"Are you serious?"

My eyes widened, realizing my actions. I sounded like a jealous little bitch. The kind that I hated. "I'm so sorry..." I took a deep breath. "I apologize. That was uncalled for."

"You're right, it's none of your damn business, but nothing happened. I told him to get out."

I stared at him.

He stared at me in return. "I ran after you, but you had already left the building."

Surprised, I stood motionless.

"I'm sorry I didn't allow you to explain."

He stepped forward and embraced me, and I knew I'd melt like butter if he kissed me.

"Jonathan, please forgive me..."

Inhaling deeply, I held his gaze. He leaned in, and our lips met. Damn! was my silent exclamation as an immediate wave of arousal swept over me, causing me to lose myself in his arms. He kissed me deeply, literally sweeping me off my feet. Effortlessly, he carried me to the bed, tossing me onto the mattress, making me feel like I had stepped right into the pages of a romance novel.

"I'm going to make love to you."

Another loud knock erupted on the door. I sat up, not knowing who it was.

"Don't answer it," he muttered.

"I bet it's Drew. He's upset. I'm sorry..." I slid out of bed and went to the door. As expected, my friend was standing at the doorway in tears.

I pulled him inside and wrapped my arms around him as his tears intensified into sobs. He couldn't stop crying. This was a side of Drew I'd never seen before.

My eyes wandered to Cody, taking in his reaction. He wore a frown, shaking his head disapprovingly at Drew's emotional state.

"I should leave," he suggested.

I nodded.

As Drew's sobs subsided, I looked at him, puzzled by his unusual demeanor. "This is so unlike you."

He sniffed, wiping his eyes.

"It's because... I'm so in love with you."

I hugged him again.

I looked at Cody. "I'll talk to you later..."

With that, he left the room. Once again, our paths diverged, and we went our separate ways. Why was it so hard to be with him? As the door closed, I turned toward Drew.

"I'm so sorry..." he whispered.

"No, you're not," I responded with a smile. "But that's okay." I kissed him on the lips. "I love you more than you realize." With that, I guided him toward the bed.

I undressed him.

After he got into bed, I undressed and slipped in beside him. I placed his head on my chest and massaged his back until he fell asleep.

As I listened to his peaceful snores, my thoughts drifted to Cody. Something always seemed to prevent us from being together.

Reflecting on the day's events, a wave of fatigue washed over me, causing my eyelids to droop slowly. Cradling Drew in my arms, I drifted into a world filled with pleasant dreams.

* * *

When I awoke the next morning, I reached out to spoon Drew, only to find an empty space. "Not again!" I groaned. Glancing at the clock, I sprang out of bed. I overslept. It was almost check-out time, and I hadn't packed yet.

"Why didn't he wake me?" I wondered.

I grabbed my suitcase and hurled it onto the bed. With little regard for organization, I tossed my clothes inside the suitcase, not worrying about neatly folding them. Once I finished packing, I dashed into the bathroom for a quick shower and to brush my teeth.

Clothed and clean, I opened the door and dragged my suitcase behind me. As I approached the elevator, I wondered if Matteo was on duty. The opening doors crushed my hopes when they revealed a female operator.

"Lobby, please," I said as I stepped in.

She pressed the button and offered a friendly smile. When we reached the ground floor, I returned her smile, thanked her, and headed toward the exit. Instead of waiting in line, I dropped the room keycard into the express check-out box and bid farewell to the "Alexander."

As I navigated the streets toward my new hotel, I realized Cody didn't know my new location. If he returned to the "Alexander" and found me gone, he'd assume I had flown back home.

I glanced at my phone—no messages from Drew or Brian. The lack of communication from my husband was a relief. "Oh, Drew..." I sighed, knowing his flight had left early, and I wouldn't see him until I returned home.

I passed a local coffee shop and noticed it was quiet. I stepped in for a simple drip coffee—nothing fancy or expensive needed.

Settling down, I pulled out my phone and looked up more information on Cody. His bio stated he was single, with no mention of being gay. This was his second and final term as a City Council Member, and he had other political ambitions. He was from Seattle and attended the University of Washington.

As I took a sip from my coffee, I noticed a figure standing on the sidewalk, looking in my direction. With little thought, I closed my eyes and massaged my neck. When I opened them, the figure, which had seemed oddly familiar, turned and walked away.

"That's strange," I mused.

I glanced back at my phone, realizing that engineering a casual encounter with Cody would be impossible unless I had more information. My only option was to return to the bathhouse to find him. With Drew out of the picture, nothing would hinder us this time.

Looking up again, I noticed a handsome Asian man seated across from me. He was smiling, his legs shifting in and out, revealing an evident erection. It wasn't large, but it was proportionate to his body. The size didn't matter to me—I appreciated all sizes.

"Hi!" I mumbled, offering him a friendly wave.

His smile broadened as he acknowledged my gesture. "I live just around the corner. Up for a quickie?"

"Are you a top?" I asked.

He grinned, gently caressing his dick. "I love fucking ass. Let's go..."

Boldly, I rose and followed him out of the coffee shop, my suitcase trailing behind. This was so unlike me, venturing off with a stranger.

We arrived at his apartment complex, which boasted a secure entry system. As we entered the elevator, he extended his hand toward me.

"I'm Kai!" he introduced himself.

"Johnathan!"

I reached over and caressed his hardness. It felt strong. I knew he'd please me completely. "You're very handsome."

"Thank you," he murmured.

The allure of his dark, exotic skin and almond-shaped eyes was captivating. His face held a unique blend of masculinity and femininity. His striking beauty left me breathless.

The elevator door opened, and I followed him to his apartment. He unlocked the door and invited me in. It was a large studio—the kitchen, living area, and bedroom were in one room. I didn't waste any time and removed my clothing. When I was naked, I kneeled, wanting to please him. My cock stood rigid, with pre-cum dripping from the slit.

"You're hot!"

"Thanks," I murmured, my eyes riveted as he disrobed.

Baring himself completely, he moved closer.

I took his cock in my mouth. It was a modest five inches but perfectly adequate for the task at hand. I lavished attention on the underside of his shaft and balls. His hygiene was impeccable. He smelled of soap as though he'd just emerged from a shower.

He stepped back, and I moaned as his dick slipped from my mouth.

"Bend over the bed," he ordered.

Reaching for the lubricant, he lubed my hole and his prick. Moments later, I felt him penetrate me. My swollen ass lips enveloped his length.

I stroked myself as he thrust inside me.

It was fast and furious, which suited me fine.

"I'm cumming!" he groaned.

His announcement spurred me on, and I stroked myself harder, climaxing simultaneously with him. He withdrew, and I turned around and licked him clean. His seed tasted delightful, smooth with a hint of pineapple.

"Thanks, man."

"You're welcome," I replied, quickly dressing. I hugged him before leaving, understanding that no further conversation was necessary.

I left his apartment building and made my way to the hotel. When I arrived, I noticed it wasn't as luxurious as the "Alexander," but it was neat. The lobby was simple and equipped with a small sitting area. After checking in, I ascended to the sixth floor in the elevator and located my room. It was compact and uninviting.

I reassured myself that it was just two nights and I was merely here to rest. My phone rang as I placed my suitcase on the bed to unpack. I retrieved it from my pocket and saw Brian's name on the screen. I took a deep breath, contemplating whether to answer. As the phone rang, I finally pressed the answer button and brought the device to my ear. I stayed quiet, waiting for my husband to start the conversation.

"Johnathan?"

"Yes."

"I'm at the Alexander Hotel."

My jaw dropped, and I stood frozen, unsure of what to say or do.

"Jonathan?"

"I'm here."

"Where are you?" he asked.

I lowered the phone, heaving a heavy sigh, not believing he had flown to Seattle.

5

The Husband

In the solitude of my hotel room, I paced back and forth after receiving an alarming phone call from my husband. He informed me he'd flown to Seattle to seek forgiveness for his betrayal.

The sudden knock on my hotel room door froze me in place. A surge of anxiety engulfed me as I acknowledged the impending confrontation. With closed eyes, I took a deep breath before approaching the door.

As I pulled it open, he stood casually in the hallway, dressed in denim, a white button-down shirt, and classic loafers.

"Johnathan," he murmured.

I motioned for him to come in. As he walked past me, I detected his cologne—the leather scent I had gifted him for his birthday.

He walked into the room, then pivoted to face me with a smile, arms outstretched for a hug. I stared at him, my face contorting into a grimace of puzzlement.

"I'm your husband. Regardless of my actions, hug me," he insisted.

His dominance took over, and I succumbed to his demands. He pulled me back in as I attempted to create distance and pressed his lips onto mine. "Brian..." I protested, struggling to break free. Yet he held me tight, deepening the kiss.

Feeling a wave of arousal, I promptly pushed away and wiped my mouth with the back of my hand. His handsome appearance, short brown hair, cleanly shaven face, and dimpled chin always left me breathless.

"I'll take a beer," he muttered, adjusting himself discreetly.

"A beer?" I mumbled, rolling my eyes at his request. I wanted to inquire if he knew the time of day, yet I chose silence, avoiding potential conflict.

Walking over to the refrigerator, I grabbed his beverage. It was a popular brand, and I knew he'd hate it. Uncapping the bottle, I handed it to him, motioning toward the couch.

As he sat, I pulled out the desk chair and positioned myself, my gaze fixed on him.

"Why aren't you sitting by me?" he questioned, not liking the distance between us.

"I'm fine here..." I responded, not trusting him. After a quiet moment, he apologized for his affair. His quick regret surprised me. I wasn't ready for that, and it caught me off guard. "You've destroyed our marriage," I stated, expecting him to elaborate further.

Brian inhaled deeply and mumbled, "I'm thirty-two years old. My life is passing by, and before I know it, I'll be in my sixties. Sex will be a thing of the past."

"Oh, Jesus... Men have sex in their sixties!" I countered, taken aback by his misguided declaration.

"You know what I mean."

"Are you saying this was a mid-life crisis?" I spat, shocked by his explanation.

"No... I won't lie to you. I was weak."

"You put us on PrEP," I stated as calmly as I could, trying to act responsibly.

He nodded in response.

"You persuaded me to do something solely for your benefit... Do you understand that?"

"I'm sorry."

I found myself speechless. Who was this person? Suddenly, he seemed so mature, taking responsibility for his actions.

With a knowing lift of his eyebrow, he declared, "I know you've had sex this weekend."

"I told you I went to the bathhouse—" I cut myself off because I didn't owe him, or anyone else, an explanation.

"I flew here to save our marriage."

His comment took my breath away. He still cared. "Your actions prompted my behavior this weekend..." I muttered.

"I know I've played a part in this, but my actions didn't force you to have sex with anyone. That was your decision."

I sat in silence, thinking deeply. Even though his words annoyed me, he was right. I didn't have to sleep around this weekend. I used his cheating as a justification.

"I will not lie and say I'm not upset because I am." He lowered his head, thinking deeply. "However, I won't deny you this time of exploration."

My breath caught in my throat. He was incredibly skilled at conversation, no doubt a trait honed by his job. As the top real estate agent in his office, outpacing everyone else in sales, he had to be. His physical attributes also helped—his tall, lean frame and green eyes were heart-melting. He could have anything he desired. "You stopped loving me," I declared, needing him to understand my pain.

"That's not true."

My eyebrows scrunched in bewilderment.

"I stopped fucking you."

I became motionless, listening to him.

"I was wrong. I should never have put someone else in your place. I realize how selfish and wrong that was of me."

Brian stood and walked over toward me. I said nothing—I just let him do what he needed. He pulled me up and embraced me again. His mouth found mine, and he kissed me deeply. He moaned, pressing his hardness against my groin.

"Forgive me..." he muttered.

I pulled away. "Brian..."

He placed his finger on my lips and shushed me. "I know you've been promiscuous. You've had sex with more than one person this weekend. I'm not stupid."

With that, he pulled my shirt over my head and kissed my neck, trailing down to my nipple. He moaned, savoring the taste of my skin.

"Brian... Stop..."

"I'm such a fool. You're so beautiful..."

Next, he unbuttoned my jeans, pulled down my underwear, and grasped my boner as it sprung forth.

"Your foreskin... drives me wild."

He kneeled, placing my dick in his mouth.

My primal desires surged. I placed my hands on his head, guiding his movements. Believe it or not, my seven-inch cock made him gag. His tongue navigated my extra skin, stimulating my sensitive tip. He moaned as a generous amount of pre-cum seeped from the slit.

"Step out of your jeans," he commanded.

I complied. I reminded myself to let go of the past, promising myself we'd discuss it further over dinner. I knew we needed to reconnect. Otherwise, we'd never move past this, and our marriage would end.

After removing my clothes, I moved to the bed. Lying down, I placed my hands behind my head and watched him undress. He took his time, almost as if he were teasing me.

I gasped, seeing his bare chest. It was devoid of hair but well-toned. He worked out, taking pride in his body. He knew he was attractive, and he flaunted it well.

Kicking off his shoes, he unbuttoned his jeans and pushed them down, letting his eight-inch cut cock spring forward.

Completely naked, he turned and reached into his backpack, pulling out leather straps.

"Brian?" I asked, surprised.

"I want you to trust me."

"Are you into bondage now?"

"The safe word is..." he glanced around the room, eyes landing on the TV mounted on the wall, "...television."

"You're tying me up?"

He nodded.

I opened my mouth, intending to halt his actions, but he silenced me. "You know I would never hurt you. Let me show you pleasure you've never felt before."

Where was this sexual kink coming from? It was a learned behavior from his coworker. Becoming upset, I told myself to let it go and trust him.

A smirk played on his lips as he climbed onto the bed, deftly securing my wrists to the bedposts. For now, he left my legs unbound from restraints. Then, positioning himself on my chest, he stroked himself, his arousal intensifying under his touch. He then rubbed it against my chest, marking me with his pre-cum that oozed from the opening.

"Open your mouth," he instructed.

As my jaw dropped, he inserted his boner inside of me. He pushed forward, shoving all eight inches down my throat—balls deep. When I choked, he pulled out.

"I love how you can deep-throat me."

He leaned forward and placed his ball sack above my mouth. I opened my mouth, and my tongue jetted out.

"Wait for my instruction."

I reminded myself of the game he was playing. He was in control, and I had to play the submissive role.

"Lick my ass," he demanded.

As I delved into his hole, I savored the unique taste that filled my senses. It was musky and earthy, leaving my taste buds tingling. The scent of soap lingered in the air, mingling with the muskiness of his body. I closed my eyes and lost myself in the moment, letting pleasure wash over me as I continued to explore his forbidden depths. I licked and sucked, exploring every inch of his ass, until he lifted himself from my mouth.

"Your tongue feels nice."

"Are you going to fuck me now?" I asked. I understood I wasn't in control and should remain quiet, but I loved his touch. He'd always been able to satiate my desires. That's why it pained me deeply when our intimate encounters became less frequent.

"Damn right, I'm going to fuck you." He untied the straps, turned me over, and, this time, tied my ankles and my wrists to the bed.

"With a dildo first."

I turned back as he jumped off the bed and removed a twelve-inch dong from his backpack.

"You brought that on the plane?" I gasped in surprise.

"No... I stopped at the sex shop."

The color and length of the dildo reminded me of the Black man that fucked me at "The Grotto." His long, thick cock pleasured me in every way.

"Where's your lube?"

"We don't need it. I was fucked this morning," I said, immediately closing my mouth in surprise at the words that had just slipped out. I braced myself for an adverse reaction, but it never came. Instead, I saw a smirk play on his face. It seemed to turn him on.

I was spread-eagle, feeling a mix of fear from losing control and excitement simultaneously. I knew he wouldn't hurt me, so I told myself to enjoy this.

He spread my ass cheeks and inspected me closely. "You have a rosebud," he said, referring to the swollen state of my ass. "I was right... You've had quite the weekend."

A wave of relief washed over me—it wasn't a prolapsed anus. After the ravishment at "The Grotto," it could have easily happened.

"It upsets me you've done this behind my back, but it turns me on that other men have used you," he whispered, then touched my swollen ass lips.

My ass puckered, and jizz oozed out. I could tell he was deep in thought because he stopped talking. I stayed silent as well, hoping the spent cum wouldn't upset him.

"Who fucked you this morning?"

"Kai," I replied.

"Asian?" Brian murmured.

"Yes."

"You love Asian men. That's hot!" he said before leaning down and licking the seeping jizz. "His cum tastes good. Reminiscent of pineapple," Brian murmured, his voice barely above a whisper. Then, with sudden intensity, his hand clamped onto the back of my neck, his fingers digging in with a frightening force. "You've been a little cum-whore this weekend!" He hissed, his words laced with an undercurrent of madness.

My eyes widened in fear. This was a side of him I didn't feel comfortable with. He was too rough. If this was role play, he was overdoing it. "Television," I replied.

He released his grip on my neck, letting his fingers gently trace the line of my back before returning to my ass cheeks. "It turns me on knowing you've taken another man's load," he admitted.

"Are you upset?" I asked softly.

"Far from it," he replied. "I want to see you with other men..."

I remained silent, unsure about my feelings toward his suggestion. Was he proposing a group encounter at the bathhouse? Soon after, I felt the tip of the dildo against my hole. I gasped, and my eyes rolled back as it penetrated me. I relaxed my muscles and allowed him to take control. He inserted about ten inches, then began moving it in and out. All I could do was moan in delight.

The feeling was heavenly, but what I yearned for was his dick. I missed the sensation of his length and girth within me. I embraced his fantasy, knowing it thrilled him.

"The dildo is going to make me cum," I moaned, hoping he'd take it out.

He removed the toy, making sure I felt every inch. As the head slipped out, I gasped at the size of it. He placed the toy in my mouth and returned his attention to my backside. I could taste Kai's pineapple-flavored jizz. It was delightful.

As I closed my eyes, Brian positioned himself on top of me and started grinding his hips. The feeling of his boner moving between my buttocks made me moan. I relaxed, knowing he was about to penetrate me without using his hands.

My eyes rolled back as his dick entered my hole. His cock pressed against my prostate, and I felt a trickle of pre-cum staining the bedspread beneath me.

The intensity was almost climactic.

"Did the guy from the bathhouse have a big dick?" he asked, his voice filled with excitement.

I tried to respond with the toy still in me but couldn't until Brian removed it. Regaining my ability to talk, I took a deep breath.

"Tell me about the man you had in your bed..." he urged.

"He had a big dick, like you," I uttered.

"What was his name?"

"Cody."

"Did he satisfy you?"

"Yes..." I moaned.

His pace increased, each thrust more powerful than the last. I moaned, groaned, and muttered explicit phrases as if possessed by the devil. What had I turned into? I felt like a porn star in some pornographic movie. I could tell he liked this new me.

"Before I give you my jizz, promise you'll take me to the bath-house."

"For what?"

"I want you to perform for me."

"With other men?"

"Yes," he whispered, kissing my neck.

His touch felt wonderful. "I promise," I gasped, craving his release once again. "Come inside me..."

"Good boy," he said, his words followed by an increase in his pace until he finally climaxed deep inside me.

I could feel his release hitting my insides. After his spasms stopped, he withdrew and unfastened the bindings. I gently rubbed my wrists, attempting to ease the discomfort caused by the tight straps.

"Use the toy and pleasure yourself," he commanded.

I crawled to the headboard and propped myself against it. Reaching down, I swiped a glob of cum on my fingers and lubricated the toy. He watched as I inserted all twelve inches. Despite feeling self-conscious at first, I found the experience arousing.

Once I felt my impending climax, I closed my eyes and threw my head back as jets of cum erupted from me. When the spasms finally ceased, Brian kissed me deeply.

"That was hot!" he exclaimed, rolling onto his back. He patted his chest, showing that he wanted me to lay my head there.

"Hold on..." I said, leaning over the bed to grab my underwear. I wiped myself clean and returned to him.

Resting my head on his upper body, I listened to his heart beating while gently massaging his chest.

"I don't expect you to understand my behavior. I'm sorry that I've hurt you. I should have been upfront from the start," he apologized.

I glanced up at him. "Our marriage will never be the same," I admitted, watching him take in my comment.

"You're right... and that's not necessarily a bad thing. Now that you've tasted what I've experienced, we should open our marriage."

His suggestion filled me with apprehension. The unknown was intimidating. I never thought I'd contemplate an open relationship. After the initial shock of his proposal, I asked, "Is that what you want?"

"Yes... Or we could consider the other alternative, divorce."

He presented two options before me. I could either adapt to his unconventional desires or confront the bitter reality of a shattered marriage. Despite the unease gnawing at me, I recognized that accepting these new terms might be less painful than experiencing the heartbreak of a failed relationship. Since he expressed his preferences, it was time for me to voice mine, "Just promise me one thing... Don't flaunt your lovers in front of me..."

"Oh, Johnny... We don't have to solve everything right now. Above all, honesty is the top priority. We'll move forward with trust," he reassured me, displaying an uncharacteristic kindness.

I nodded, caressing his toned chest. My fingers traveled down his abdomen, and I played with his pubic hair. His arousal was immediate, responding to my sensual touch. I caressed his shaft back and forth.

"I love you," he confessed.

His words made me pause. I reciprocated his sentiment. "I love you too." We had spent so many years together. Despite his domineering nature, the thought of life without him was heartbreaking.

"You made the right decision," he whispered, pulling me in for a tighter hug. "I wouldn't be able to go on without you..."

"If we're going to the bathhouse tonight, we must eat early. I can't get fucked on a full stomach," I replied, forcing the troubling thoughts about my husband out of my mind.

"That's fine."

As I continued to rest my head on his chest, I found myself deep in thought. Had I changed too? Did I now desire sex with other men? Fear crept in as I pondered these unsettling questions.

* * *

We dined at an Italian restaurant called the "Hungry Italian." We found the restaurant's entrance discreetly tucked away in a waterfront alleyway. There were no signs showing it was a restaurant other than a pink door. Once we sat down, the server informed us that the "Duomo" inspired the door's color.

We started with antipasti. Brian had linguine alle vongole for the main course, and I opted for a simple salad. Despite its simplicity, it was delicious.

Halfway through the meal, Brian's phone rang. He glanced at the screen and looked at me with a severe expression.

"I need to take this," he said.

"Who is it?" I asked.

"It's business," he responded.

I nodded as he took the call. He stood and walked away from our table. He seemed happy to hear from the person on the other end. I shrugged it off and let it go. When he didn't return, I pulled out my phone and dialed Drew's number. I was worried about him and wanted to ensure he was okay.

He picked up immediately.

"Hi, Drew!"

"Hello, Johnathan," he replied in a monotone voice.

His disposition was hard to read. It almost seemed as if he was upset.

"How are you doing?"

"I'm unpacking. I'm fine. How's Seattle?" he queried.

I paused, thinking deeply. "Brian showed up this morning."

"Oh?"

"He came for forgiveness."

There was a long pause on the other end. I waited for him to respond, but when he didn't, I continued.

"Drew?"

"I'm listening..."

"Brian will be back shortly, so I don't have time to go into everything. I'm calling to see how you're doing. You left this morning without saying goodbye."

"I didn't want to wake you."

"That was considerate, but it would have been nice to hold you before you headed to the airport." I paused before continuing. "What happened between us felt good..."

"Johnathan?"

"I think I love you too..." I whispered. He interrupted me just as I gathered my thoughts to speak again.

"Have you forgiven Brian?" he asked. My breath hitched at the sudden shift in conversation. It was as if he hadn't heard the heartfelt confession I had just made.

"Johnathan?"

"I guess."

"You guess?"

"I haven't said, 'I forgive you,' but we're moving on..."

"What do you mean?"

"We're not letting his affair destroy us." I waited for Drew to say something more, but he remained quiet. "Our marriage is now open."

After a long silence, Drew's voice suddenly erupted. "That fucking bastard! I can't believe him!"

"Drew?" I muttered, taken aback by his outburst.

"He always gets what he wants. It's all about him. He treats you poorly, and you either don't see it or don't care," he ranted.

"If he's selfish, it's likely because of his upbringing," I tried to reason, my voice softening.

"Stop making excuses for him!" Drew snapped back. "Do you think this is the first time he's fucked around on you?"

"I'm in a restaurant..." I whispered.

He continued berating me.

Letting out a weary sigh, I lifted my gaze. My eyes landed on a man in the lounge. He was flailing his hands about wildly, clearly agitated about something. As I squinted to get a better look, the figure caught sight of me and quickly disappeared behind a wall. There was something eerily familiar about him—he reminded me of Drew.

"Where are you?" I questioned.

No response.

"Drew?"

"I told you. I'm home, unpacking..."

"I must be losing it... I thought I just saw you..."

"Johnathan?"

"It's nothing. Forget it." I took a deep breath to compose myself. "I'm unsure if this open relationship will save or ruin us."

"You're a fool."

"Really, Drew?"

After a long pause, contemplating his words, I moved on. "I tried to tell you last night. The way you..." I lowered my voice. "The way you made love to me blew me away... I've never felt pleasure like that before."

"Oh, Johnathan... That makes me happy hearing you say that."

I looked up and saw Brian looking down at me, listening to our conversation. "Hey, I've got to run. I'll talk to you soon." I ended the call and smiled at Brian.

"Who was that?" he questioned.

"Ah... Cody. The man I met at the bathhouse." I lied because I didn't want Brian to know Drew and I had been intimate.

"Delete his number now."

"What?"

"You heard me. DELETE IT NOW, OR I WILL!"

"What the hell? Keep your voice down..."

Brian reached forward. "Give me your goddamn phone!"

"You're causing a scene." His aggressive behavior was coming out. I went to my recent calls. I deleted everything on record, pretending to delete Cody's number. "There... It's done," I said, showing him my phone.

"Thank you."

I didn't respond and sat motionless, questioning his demanding ways. I picked up my fork and resumed eating my salad. This wasn't a good start to rekindling our marriage.

After lunch, we strolled around "Pike Place Market" and the "Seattle Art Museum." Afterward, we paused for coffee. Apart from the phone incident, we had a wonderful afternoon. Brian dedicated a lot of time to me, solidifying our bond.

On entering the hotel, I undressed and headed to the bathroom to get "fuck ready" when Brian asked me to wait because he had something for me to sign.

"What is it?"

"Life insurance," he replied.

"We already have a policy."

"I've increased the amount," he explained.

I watched as he opened his backpack and pulled out an envelope. He removed the paperwork, which he unfolded and placed on the desk. He handed me a pen and instructed me on where to sign it. Strangely, he hadn't consulted me, but I wasn't about to question him and ruin our evening. After signing, I asked, "Where's your policy?"

"I've already signed mine," he replied.

"I have to sign it!"

"I accidentally left it at home. You can sign it when we get back," he assured, and then reached for my cock, diverting my thoughts from the policy. "Can I pee on you?" he asked out of the blue with a broad grin.

Taken aback, I shook my head. "What the hell? Have you lost your mind?"

"It's fun!" he tried to convince me.

I was once again questioning where all this came from. His coworker must be pretty kinky.

"Come on... Let me pee on you."

By this point, my cock had hardened. The movement of my fore-skin back and forth over my dick head was arousing me. I shook my head, giving up. "Sure... Whatever..." I muttered under my breath. By this point, nothing about him surprised me anymore.

Brian removed his hand from my dick and led me into the bath-room. He gestured to the tub.

I stepped inside.

"Kneel and open your mouth."

Obediently, I got on my knees as he unbuttoned his jeans. His cock was already hard, clearly excited by the thought of peeing on me. I knew some men found pleasure in it. I didn't understand the appeal, but I'd try it for my husband's sake.

Brian stroked his cock. I could see pre-cum glistening at the tip.

My lips parted at the sight of his erection. His cock had always turned me on and satisfied me beyond measure. Feeling his dominance over me, I touched myself. The submissive role strangely aroused me, even though I constantly questioned why. But this wasn't the time or place for introspection.

A hot stream erupted from his dick, splattering on my face. I flinched initially, taken aback by the smell and the warmth against my skin.

"Open wide!" Brian commanded.

I complied, opening my mouth as he directed the stream toward it. The salty taste surprised me. It wasn't unpleasant, but I liked it because it was Brian's urine. I was sure I couldn't stomach anyone else's.

Knowing not to swallow it, I let it flow out of my mouth and down my chest. I found the entire experience strangely arousing and ended up stroking myself.

"Swallow the last bit," Brian instructed as the stream diminished.

I leaned forward to catch the last spurts. Holding the urine in my mouth, I waited for his command.

"Swallow it."

I told myself not to overthink it, do it! And so, I swallowed. To my surprise, it wasn't as bad as I'd expected. It was not something I'd do regularly, but it was an exciting way to start the evening.

"Next time, I'll show you what a 'golden douche' is."

"I know what that is... It's time for you to leave," I grinned, gesturing toward the door.

He smirked. "Tonight's going to be fun."

I watched him exit the room and close the door behind him. Turning on the shower, I washed the urine off my body with soap and rinsed my mouth with warm water. Standing under the shower, I had a lot to think about. Was my husband going to pimp me out tonight? The idea oddly turned me on. Then my thoughts turned to Cody. Would I see him again? With Brian in town, there was no time for anyone else. The thought saddened me.

Then, thoughts of Matteo and Ciro flooded my mind. I yearned to be in their company again, to engage in our playful antics. But with Brian's presence, the likelihood of that happening was slim, too.

Then there was Drew. A surge of longing washed over me at the thought of him. I desired to continue our encounter, but I knew Brian would never consent to it, even though we had an open relationship now.

In a surprising character twist, I concluded I'd have to resort to dishonesty or never be with Drew again. It was uncharacteristic of me, but I recognized it as a necessary evil.

Brian had never explicitly stated that we had to disclose our sexual exploits, and I had no intention of initiating such a conversation. My private escapades would remain just that—private.

Turning the lever, I diverted the water to the handheld sprayer attached to my douche hose and prepared myself for what was to come.

6

The Happy Ending

Brian clasped my hand as we meandered toward the bathhouse, deepening our connection. I was growing increasingly fond of this softer side of him. This gentle moment opened discussions about his betrayal, our future, and, most importantly, what he expected from me tonight. After Brian suggested we open our marriage, I agreed to accompany him to appease his desires.

Upon arriving at the bathhouse, I pushed open the door, and the soothing aroma of eucalyptus surrounded us.

My eyes immediately sought the check-in counter, landing on Andy, the attendant shielded by plexiglass. Noticing us, his gaze flickered with intrigue, trying to discern the nature of our relationship.

"Hello, Andy!" I called out warmly.

"Johnathan," he acknowledged, shifting his focus to my husband. "This is Brian."

Brian's eyes moved to Andy, who confidently displayed his toned torso. Brian's attention momentarily lingered on the distinct bulge in Andy's shorts. Following an unintentional adjustment, Andy subtly accentuated it, drawing an admiring look from Brian. His dick looked enormous, almost too big to be real.

"Damn... Interested in fucking ass?" Brian inquired, a note of admiration in his voice.

His directness caught me off guard, and my eyes widened in astonishment. "He's not allowed," I promptly interjected, recalling that I had asked the same question during my initial visit.

"That's rather unfortunate," Brian remarked with a sly smirk, continuing to engage Andy through the glass barrier.

"I might be able to slip away," Andy smirked, his tone hinting at mischief.

"But you mentioned it was against the rules," I pointed out, confused.

"The boss is away today," he replied nonchalantly.

I nodded, acknowledging his point.

"How would you like to pay?" Andy then inquired.

"In cash," Brian said promptly, taking out his wallet.

After handling the payment, Andy gave us towels, condoms, and locker keys on bungee cords.

Handing me my share, Brian turned back to Andy with a daring request, asking him to lower his shorts. Astonishingly, he complied, displaying his impressive 8-inch erection.

"Remarkable," Brian murmured under his breath. "I'd love to see that in my husband's ass."

I noticed the "Prince Albert" piercing adorning the tip of Andy's cock. "Oh, definitely not with that!" I objected, pointing at the metallic ring in shock.

"It's removable," Andy assured us.

"Find us later," Brian proposed in a hushed tone, a blend of excitement and provocation evident in his voice.

Andy's grin widened, heightening the suspense.

Feeling anxious, I managed a tentative smile, reluctant to disrupt the moment.

"Have fun," Andy called out.

"Thanks," Brian replied, signaling for me to follow. He pushed the lever down, opening the door to the lounge, and we stepped into the next phase of our evening.

Naked men drinking beverages filled the room, sitting on stools, chaise lounges, and couches. A George Michael video played on the giant television screen. With his black leather attire, Cesar haircut, and imperial beard, he belted out lyrics about "Fast Love." I scanned the area, searching for a familiar face, but to my dismay, none greeted me.

We left the lounge and entered the locker room, where men were undressing, each getting ready for a night of intimate encounters. We found our locker amidst the rows and began undressing as the sound of men bathing in the showers filled the room. Glancing over at Brian, a thought crossed my mind—had he ever experienced a bathhouse? It was a topic that had never surfaced in our conversations. Intrigued, I couldn't resist asking him directly if he had. Brian nodded, leaving me curious yet again—his expression gave away nothing.

Before I could step out of my jeans and underwear, he suddenly reached out and grasped my dick, moving it back and forth in a slow, rhythmic motion. Startled by this unexpected gesture, I asked, "What are you doing?"

He responded, "Drawing them in."

Immediately, my cock became hard. I chuckled, playing along with his light-hearted banter. However, deep down, I understood the seriousness behind his words—he wanted me to be intimate with multiple men. It didn't instill fear in me, but made me question his motives. It was as if I was dealing with a stranger, not the husband I had known for many years. We undressed, wrapped our towels around our waists, and closed our lockers.

"Let's hit the showers," Brian murmured, tucking something that glinted into his towel's fold.

"What's that?" I asked, curiosity piqued.

"Poppers," he replied.

The object didn't resemble any bottle I knew of. But before I could probe further, he ushered me toward the shower. I hung my towel on a hook while Brian tossed his onto a bench, concealing the mysterious object.

Once inside, Brian turned on one of the showerheads. Then he faced me and nudged me toward the floor.

"Suck me."

Confused, I arched an eyebrow.

"Do as I say."

Submissively, I took his impressive eight-inch cock inside my mouth. I knew how much he reveled in my oral skills, mainly because I could accommodate his full length—a feat many men found challenging. I dedicated myself to providing him with the utmost pleasure. The pre-cum emerging from him signified his arousal.

"Does anyone want a blow job?" Brian announced loudly.

I momentarily paused my actions to glance at the three men approaching us.

"Service them," Brian whispered, nudging me to heed his instructions. Withdrawing his dick from my mouth, he made way for them.

My eyes met them as I felt the anticipation in the air. Their hard bodies and confident demeanor made me feel slightly nervous. As I leaned forward, I locked eyes with the closest man.

Focusing on him, I studied the contours of his body, the way his muscles flexed, and the determination etched on his face. As I reached for his hard-on, I felt the firmness, taking a moment to appreciate it. Running my fingers softly along the length, I saw his well-groomed pubes that adorned it.

Gently brushing my lips against the head, I felt the man's prick pulsating, a testament to his arousal. I moved my head back and forth, sucking and caressing his cock with my tongue. I could taste a hint of pre-cum, which only fueled my desire to please him further.

"Cum in his mouth!" Brian ordered.

The man pulled out and started stroking his cock. The other two guys stepped closer as their ejaculations began building. I sucked them, knowing I'd be taking all three loads simultaneously.

Loud moans escaped from the first guy.

I turned to him, and he came into my mouth, the warmth spreading as I swallowed. As the following two jets landed on my face, I licked my lips, craving more of him. The second man moaned, so I shifted my focus to him just as he released his load. The first jet hit my cheek, but I caught the next two in my mouth, the streams hitting the back of my throat. After he finished, I swallowed and turned my attention to the third guy.

His jizz shot in multiple streams, forcibly striking my face.

"Open wider!" He moaned.

I obeyed, and the next three jets shot into my mouth. His jizz was watery, rushing out fast, so I swallowed it quickly.

"Hot!" Brian muttered, stroking himself.

The three guys thanked me and turned to shower. I looked at Brian with the residue of jizz on my face, and he smirked back at me. I could tell it was a turn-on.

"Get cleaned up."

I nodded in understanding. As I washed my face, I turned and noticed all the men in the locker room staring with interest. It was clear they wished they had joined in. Dispensing soap from the container, I proceeded to bathe. When I looked up, I caught Andy, the bathhouse employee, watching intently. He had witnessed me servicing all the men. I waved in a friendly manner. He grimaced, bent down, picked up a bucket of cleaning supplies, and walked away. Realizing that he was upset, I felt terrible but recognized the issue was his, not mine.

Upon completing his shower, Brian said he was going to dry off. I nodded and continued bathing. The warm water provided a soothing sensation on my skin. I applied soap to my groin and ass, preparing for the evening. Once finished, I turned off the showerhead and stepped out.

As I was drying off beside Brian, my breath hitched when I saw Cody entering the locker room. He was incognito, donned in a baseball cap with his head down. Panic set in, leaving me unsure of what to do. I knew I couldn't approach him, so I nudged Brian and gestured toward the pool and jacuzzi area.

"I'm still wet," he protested.

"Come on..." I coaxed, nudging him onward. He gazed at me in confusion, to which I replied with a mischievous grin, saying that I was horny.

A smirk spread across his face as he processed my words. I watched as he carefully tucked away the object he was holding into the folds of his towel. Upon closer inspection, I realized it wasn't a bottle of poppers. It was a switchblade.

Brian caught the astonished look on my face as I stared downwards. "There's some real nutcases here," he remarked, motioning toward the exit.

As confusion swept over me, I turned back and saw Cody glancing in our direction. I cursed under my breath, dreading his potential approach. Without Brian's awareness, I gestured discreetly, urging Cody to keep his distance. Cody, however, remained fixated on Brian, oblivious to my silent plea. When he finally looked at me, I mouthed, "Stay away..."

Cody didn't acknowledge me. There was no head nod, nothing. He opened his locker and started undressing.

"Where do you want to go?" I asked, turning back to Brian as he walked toward the exit.

"Not sure... Let's check it out."

Entering the pool area, I turned to find him scanning the room for potential playmates. I knew he wasn't looking for himself—he was searching for me. Tonight, it was my role to fulfill his fantasy. In the absence of a plan, I suggested going to the "Fuck" room to avoid Cody.

Brian nodded in agreement, not seeing anyone to play with. As we started toward the exit, he paused momentarily, distracted by a man with a nine-inch cock receiving head. Nervously, I nudged him forward while glancing over my shoulder to check on Cody. He wasn't behind us.

Upon entering the dimly lit "Fuck" room, I strained my eyes to adjust to the darkness that shrouded the area. The room was brimming with naked men, their bodies melding together in the low light.

While scanning the room for potential sex partners, I immediately noticed a captivating scene unfolding on one of the platforms. A man was being fisted. Lying on his back with his legs hoisted in the air, two men took turns punching his asshole with their fists. They weren't being gentle. They were being forceful, and the man on the receiving end reveled in it. It was too intense, so I turned away.

I spotted my Italian friend Matteo in one corner of the room, meticulously securing a blindfold over his brother's eyes.

Once the blindfold was secure, Matteo rewarded Ciro with a deep kiss, followed by a playful tug on his prick. Unsure of what was happening, I watched intently, hoping Brian wouldn't pull us away.

Ciro reclined on a platform, his body language showing eagerness for the sensual journey that was about to unfold. Meanwhile, Matteo gestured for a man nearby to come closer. Their heads bent in conversation, and moments later, the man climbed onto the platform and straddled Ciro. As he lowered himself onto Ciro's throbbing cock, a wave of excitement ran through me.

"What about them?"

Brian nodded in agreement.

I knew Brian would keep his distance, allowing me to inform Matteo that the man watching was my husband and he shouldn't acknowledge me. We would pretend to be strangers. Despite the language barrier, Matteo would understand and play along. "Wait here," I instructed Brian. To my surprise, he nodded, allowing me to take control of the situation.

Approaching Matteo, I silenced him with a look. Then, leaning in, I whispered my husband was here and we needed to act as if we didn't know each other.

"Si…"

"Can I be next?" I pointed at Ciro.

With a nod and a smile, Matteo looked at me with eyes full of love. I leaned in for a warm embrace, and then our lips merged in a passionate French kiss.

Whispering, I murmured, "After I'm done with Ciro, I want you to live out your fantasy."

"I… I don't understand."

"Be intimate with him," I clarified. "Sit on his cock. Make love to him."

"No, no, no…" Matteo responded, momentarily taken aback.

"I know this is your wish. This is your chance…" I urged him. "Ciro has a blindfold on—he won't know it's you."

"My brother will be upset…"

"I'll keep him preoccupied."

As Matteo weighed the situation, a look of realization crossed his face. "I understand," he admitted. Moments later, Matteo gestured to the man Ciro was pleasuring to step off the platform. Despite the man's disappointment, he complied with Matteo's request.

Matteo beckoned me to the stand.

I stepped onto the stage and positioned myself over Ciro. Glancing back at Brian, I smiled. He returned my grin, stroking his cock in anticipation. I spread my ass cheeks, and he nodded, signaling to proceed. Acknowledging his gesture, I turned back around. I knew he was in a state of ecstasy and wouldn't question the situation.

As I welcomed Ciro's eager cock inside me, a sigh of pleasure escaped my lips. The reunion was blissful—his hard length filled me. We started moving in sync, and I savored every inch.

Feeling Matteo near my ass, I glanced back and saw him licking Ciro's balls as they bounced back and forth. I knew Ciro would cum soon. Despite the temptation to fuck him harder for his release, it didn't belong to me.

I dismounted Ciro and signaled to Matteo that it was his turn. As he straddled his brother, I leaned down and kissed Ciro. Engaged in a deep French kiss, I prevented him from removing his blindfold, allowing Matteo to savor the experience fully.

Breaking away from Ciro's lips, I turned to Matteo. Seeing the pleasure in his eyes, I knew this would be a moment he'd remember forever. This was something he had yearned for. He loved his brother deeply, a love that transcended the bounds of typical brotherly affection.

The joy on Matteo's face was pure bliss. Moments later, he exhaled softly, attempting to muffle his moans as he approached his orgasm. Gently stroking his uncut prick, his movements sped up. In sync, Ciro increased his pace. Within a few seconds, jets of cum erupted from Matteo's cock. I caught them in my mouth. Not long after, Ciro's cries filled the room as he released in his brother's ass.

After Ciro's spasms subsided, Matteo's eyes met mine, reflecting gratitude for the unforgettable experience I had provided.

I gestured for Matteo to dismount Ciro as Brian approached with two guys in tow. He directed me to get on all fours. I embraced Matteo and whispered to tell Ciro to act as if he didn't know me.

"Si. Si..." was his response.

I got into the position. The raised platform felt like a stage, and all the men not engaged in sex turned toward me. The man with the biggest dick kneeled behind me and began fucking my ass while the other guy placed his cock inside my mouth.

Raising my hips, I took the man's length deeply. Meanwhile, the man thrusting into my mouth did so roughly, but I didn't choke since I could deep-throat him. I noticed Matteo whispering to his brother from the corner of my eye. In response, Ciro removed his blindfold, looking at me with concern.

Brian stepped forward, eager to take part. He pushed the guy fucking me away. As he started his movements, my head shot back in pain. When I turned around to stop him, I heard a familiar voice.

"Let me have a turn."

I saw Cody motioning for Brian to step back. In shock, Brian moved away, allowing Cody to take his place. As I glanced at Cody, disappointment clouded his eyes. I remained silent, knowing that any words or actions would only clarify the situation to my husband.

"Lie on your back," I heard Cody say.

I flipped over, raising my legs. As Cody entered me, he immediately started moving rhythmically, leading me into a state of ecstasy. When I caught my breath, I glanced back at Brian. A surge of emotions played across his face—jealousy, hurt, and anger all mingled together. Without uttering a word, he mouthed, "Fuck you" and flipped me the bird. The old Brian, with all his insecurities, had resurfaced.

Cody continued to fuck me with passion, trailing kisses along my neck. I let out a gasp as Cody's impressive length and girth pleasured me. In a whisper, he expressed his concern, insisting that I shouldn't be having sex with all these men.

In response, I murmured that my husband was behind him and that he wanted me to do this. The revelation halted his movements.

"That's your husband?"

"Yes."

"He has a knife," Cody whispered.

"I know…"

"I followed you in here because he's up to something."

Now that Cody had ceased his movements, I knew Brian would question the situation. "Keep fucking," I whispered, my gaze shifting toward Brian as he searched for a replacement. "Otherwise, he'll find someone else."

Cody kissed me upon hearing my revelation and started thrusting again.

I pulled away to catch my breath and saw men gathering, each waiting their turn. My heart clenched at the sight of Andy at the front of the line.

His disgust unnerved me, and I was at a loss for what to do. I didn't want him close, but I could do nothing to prevent it. I noticed his "Prince Albert" piercing was still in place.

Suddenly, everything became overwhelming. The memories of my weekend replayed in my mind, bringing back flashes of the anonymous encounters I'd experienced. The "Bathhouse," the "Gloryhole," and "Patrick's" lounge were vivid in my recollection. There were so many men. My stomach churned as I realized the extent of my overzealous actions.

Why did I agree to come here? I should have said no to Brian, I thought. I wanted a monogamous relationship, not an open marriage. Seeing the anger in my husband's eyes, I braced myself for some form of punishment. This was a man I now feared—I didn't recognize him anymore.

As Cody's lips met mine, I withdrew and whispered for him to get me out of there.

"Okay…"

The thought of how Brian might respond to Cody's actions crossed my mind, but I didn't care. Meanwhile, the line of men transformed into a crowd, obscuring Brian from my view.

Anticipating Cody's orgasm, I elevated my legs further. Seconds later, his groans erupted as he released his cum deep inside me. I grasped his backside and continued to kiss him until he pulled away.

A burst of light filled the room.

As my eyes adjusted, I saw the crowd forming around two men in a violent struggle. One of them had a knife that glinted in the low light. Squinting, I recognized them as Drew, my friend and coworker, and Andy, the bathhouse employee.

I gasped as Andy swung the knife toward Drew, narrowly missing his face. Drew reached for the knife, but Andy swung it again. This time, it connected with Drew's shoulder. He shouted out an expletive, backing away.

Cody and I separated.

Seeing that no one was stepping in to break the men apart, Cody took matters into his own hands. He darted forward, swiftly disarming Andy and throwing the knife on the platform.

Rushing toward Drew, my mind spun from his sudden and unexpected appearance. As he collapsed to the floor, I dropped to my knees, applying pressure to his wound to stop the bleeding.

Looking at Drew's face, I saw his eyes flutter shut, slipping into unconsciousness. "Someone call 911!" I shouted.

Cody handed Andy over to Ciro and kneeled beside me, applying pressure on Drew's laceration.

"He's got the knife!" came a shout from somewhere in the crowd.

When I looked up, I saw someone running away. At that moment, the bathhouse lights flickered on, and I recognized the retreating figure—my husband, Brian.

"Let me go... I've done nothing wrong." Andy protested, squirming and trying to escape from Ciro's tight grip.

"Explain yourself," Ciro demanded in his Italian accent, his voice filled with anger.

"I was protecting Johnathan."

"I don't believe you."

"Let him explain!" Cody interrupted.

"Brian was going to stab him."

"Oh, my God..." I murmured. Brian's retreating figure confirmed this.

Turning toward me, Cody explained, "He's telling the truth."

I stared at Cody in disbelief, feeling surreal that my husband had tried to kill me. Was this reality, or was I dreaming?

"You're safe. I'm sure he's already exiting the building," Cody explained, trying to calm my nerves. "He's gone now."

"This is unreal," I murmured, deep in thought.

"Jonathan?" Drew moaned, awakening.

I snapped to attention upon hearing my name. Glancing down, I noticed my friend's eyes fluttering open. Relief washed over me and tears cascaded down my cheeks.

"Johnathan?"

"I'm here..." I breathed, watching Drew's eyes flicker from me to Cody. However, when he looked at Andy, he recoiled, his face contorting with fear.

"He's not going to hurt you," I uttered.

Drew's speech conveyed mumbling and fear. "I tackled him. He had a knife..."

"It was Brian's..."

Drew's eyes narrowed, struggling to understand my words. "Andy was protecting me," I explained as the sirens grew louder in the distance.

"Someone give me a towel!" Cody yelled, his eyes scanning the crowd.

Matteo stepped forward and unwrapped the cloth from his waist. Cody took it and pressed it against Drew's wound to stop the bleeding.

Andy kneeled beside Drew.

"I took the knife from Brian," he clarified, his words aimed at dissipating the confusion on Drew's face.

"He was going to stab Johnathan?"

Andy nodded.

My mind reeled from everything that had happened in the past 24 hours. I thought Brian had come to save our marriage, but instead, he came to kill me. I remembered the increase in the life insurance, which confirmed everything.

"Everyone, step back," a paramedic ordered, entering the room.

As I stood, I saw three men, one notably handsome and muscular, rushing toward us. He seemed to observe the scene with interest, probably not used to responding to emergencies in a bathhouse.

He kneeled next to Drew, examining the cut. Then he opened his tackle box and removed everything he needed while his fellow medic took Drew's vital signs. After cleaning the wound and applying butterfly bandages, he covered it with a gauze dressing.

"Do you have any other injuries?" he asked, looking over Drew's body.

"No... I'm fine," Drew insisted.

The paramedic glanced at his coworkers. "Place him on the gurney..."

"I'm not going anywhere!"

The paramedic raised an eyebrow in confusion. When Drew shook his head, the medic turned to Cody, recognizing him.

"Mr. Cromwell, your friend needs..."

"I refuse treatment." Drew blurted out.

Cody and I locked eyes. The paramedic knew his last name and, along with it, his job title—City Council Member. Everyone openly acknowledged his identity now.

I turned, noticing the paramedic's eyes wandering lower, landing on Cody's cock. Moments later, I saw the bulge pressing against his slacks.

"We'll look after him," Cody murmured.

"Alright," the paramedic replied, giving Cody an interested look.

As I turned back to Cody, I couldn't help but notice his excitement. His prick stood rigid, pulsating with anticipation.

"We've done all we can here," the paramedic said as he collected his supplies, addressing his colleagues.

When he stood, he covered his erection. His gaze fell back on Cody.

"Believe it or not, I enjoy watching the City Council meetings on TV."

Cody responded with a flirty grin and handshake. "Thank you..."

"You're welcome!"

After they shared a lingering look, the paramedic turned and left the room. I saw Cody checking out his backside. The medic's ass was firm and round, a result of long hours at the gym.

I turned my attention back to Drew, looking into his eyes. "You're supposed to be in San Francisco!"

"I never left," he confessed.

"You never left?" I squinted to comprehend his words. "Have you been following me?" I asked, a knot forming in my stomach.

"What are you talking about?" he replied, confusion clouding his features.

"Were you at 'Patrick's' lounge?"

"No..."

"It was your husband!" Matteo interjected, his English broken. He stepped forward, caressing my backside. "I saw him staring at you. When I said excuse me, he stepped aside anxiously as if he was doing something wrong."

"I remember you telling me..." In shock, I turned my gaze back to Drew, my heart pounding.

"The only time I followed you was at the Italian restaurant. That's it. Why are you asking these questions?"

"Someone's been stalking me."

"Oh..."

Closing my eyes, I allowed the truth to sink in. Brian hadn't arrived this morning—he had caught a plane immediately after I confronted him about his affair. "Damn it!" I burst out, shaking my head in disbelief. It was Brian all this time. This realization echoed in my mind until another thought struck me with the force of a blow. He was still involved with his lover. His apology, his feigned remorse, was all an act. Brian knew I was going to divorce him, so he realized he had to kill me, or he'd lose his fortune.

"The cops are on their way," Andy said, his eyes filled with anxiety.

"I bet the reporters won't be far behind," Cody muttered.

I turned to him, noticing his contemplative expression. It was clear he was pondering our next move. "How about we hide in your room?" I proposed.

"Yes..." He glanced at Andy. "Please, don't let them know where we are. If this leaks out, my career is finished."

Andy agreed with a nod.

Reaching out, I clasped Andy's hand. "I owe you an apology... I thought you hated me."

He shook his head in bewilderment. "No... I was just frustrated," Andy explained. "You didn't want to have sex with me."

I embraced him. "Thank you," I said as he held me tightly, feeling my naked body against his. "I'm sorry we didn't have time to get to know one another..."

"You better get going."

"Thank you for everything," Cody murmured, shaking Andy's hand.

Once we finished saying our goodbyes, Cody and I helped Drew stand, and we started walking toward the private rooms. Minutes later, the bathhouse lights went off, replaced by a reddish glow that bathed the hallways, returning them to their alluring atmosphere.

We arrived at the room.

"Jonathan?"

Upon hearing Matteo's voice, I turned to see him standing naked beside me. Cody took Drew from my grasp, understanding that Matteo sought some alone time.

"Go be with your friend," he muttered.

Drew motioned for me to leave, and they stepped into the room, shutting the door behind them. I faced Matteo, extending my arms, and we embraced firmly.

"You left without a goodbye."

"I'm sorry," I whispered.

"Thank you for granting my wish."

I smiled in understanding. He was talking about his brother. "I know you love him. Make him understand your feelings." After deep thought, Matteo nodded, knowing I was right.

"Am I wrong for loving him?"

I thought deeply, finding it difficult to provide a straightforward answer. Matteo was genuinely kind-hearted. Who was I to judge what was right or wrong? "I don't know," I admitted. "Seeing your love for him, how could that be wrong?"

"Si. Si…"

As Matteo pulled me into another embrace, I felt his arousal pressing against me. Looking down, I couldn't suppress a smile. "You gave your towel away." His beautiful, uncut cock was visibly excited. Unable to resist, I gently caressed him, finding the motion of sliding his foreskin back and forth incredibly arousing.

"I'm so happy we met," he murmured.

"Me too!"

He glanced down, noticing the pre-cum oozing from the tip of his prick. With a hint of desire in his Italian accent, he whispered, "You turn me on… Can we be together one more time?"

Smiling, I wiped the pre-cum off with my finger and tasted it—it was divine. Bowing my head, I deeply contemplated the situation with the two men waiting for me. Realizing that Cody and I lived in different cities clarified that our relationship could only extend to friendship. Thinking of Drew, I felt confident he would understand.

"Yes. I'd like that."

Matteo smiled and took my hand. "Let's find a secluded place."

I allowed him to lead me to an area where we wouldn't get interrupted. Once there, I embraced him. Matteo had always pleasured me, so I wanted to return the favor this time. I lowered him onto a platform and lifted his legs.

"Johnathan?"

"Hush… This is my gift to you."

I leaned forward, and my tongue shot out, licking around his hole. It puckered in excitement. The thick hair around it was massive. He smelled of cum, and the scent drove me into ecstasy. My tongue delved deep into him.

"Si, Johnathan… Scopami il buco del culo con la lingua."

I could taste his brother's jizz. As it trickled out, I swallowed, savoring it.

"Si. Si... Your tongue feels incredible. Kiss me now..." Matteo sighed, wanting my lips on his.

I pulled away and kissed him deeply. As I did this, I inserted my cock inside his well-lubricated ass and made love to him, channeling all the passion I could muster.

He gasped for breath in between our kisses. "Oh, Johnathan..."

My excitement continued to build until my cum released inside him. As I cried out, he held me tightly, not wanting it to end. After my body stopped spasming, I placed his uncut prick inside my mouth and sucked him. He was so excited he came quickly.

"Il mio sperma sta arrivando."

I closed my eyes, memorizing the taste and texture of him. Before swallowing it, Matteo stopped me.

"Let me taste..." He moaned.

I kissed him passionately. Then we both swallowed, sharing it. As I pulled away, I stared deep into his eyes. This was it. It was time to say goodbye. "They're waiting for me, Matteo. Take care..."

"Oh, Johnathan... I'm going to miss you so..."

I leaned in, our lips meeting once more in a tender kiss. Reluctantly pulling away, I rose to my feet, committing every detail of his presence to memory. My heart ached with love for Matteo, and realizing that our shared moments had ended was almost too much to bear. Our souls had intertwined in the brief time we had known each other. A tear escaped my eye as I wrapped the towel around my waist. "Call me some time," I murmured and turned to leave, sparing him the sight of my sorrow. Casting one last glance over my shoulder, I saw him walking in the opposite direction, his beautiful, olive-skinned backside glowing in the distance. Despite the ache in my heart, seeing his sculpted body made me smile.

Leisurely strolling through the corridors, I observed men searching for their release. The bathhouse appeared to have returned to its usual rhythm, and in no time, I was back at Cody's room.

With a gentle tap, I opened the door and saw them sitting beside each other, naked, engrossed in conversation. Upon entering, I playfully inquired, "Do I need to introduce you guys again?" remembering their meeting in the hotel room.

Drew responded with a warm smile, turning toward Cody. "No... we've gotten acquainted," he said, his eyes sparkling with fondness toward him.

Cody leaned forward, pressing a gentle kiss on Drew's lips, before rising and removing my towel from around my waist. His gaze then drifted down to my flaccid cock.

"I had sex," I offered, preempting his unspoken question. Greeted with silence, I felt compelled to elaborate. "I hoped you'd understand."

Exchanging a knowing look, Drew and Cody's smiles widened before they turned back to me.

"It's what we expected," Drew stated, his tone filled with understanding.

"Now, we're all friends here," Cody said, his nod reinforcing our sense of unity.

I shared my appreciation for their understanding and acceptance.

Cody moved closer to Drew, placing a hand on his shoulder and positioning his dick just inches from his face.

Catching sight of it, Drew watched as it hardened.

"It has a mind of its own..." Cody murmured with a smirk.

Drew leaned forward and took Cody in his mouth. My jaw dropped—not in jealousy, but in surprise. Cody didn't recoil. He let it happen.

"I know you and Drew are more than friends now," Cody said. "I understand my place and want to be part of this."

Drew pulled away from Cody and looked at me for permission. I nodded, approving of the direction this was heading. I loved them both, so I consented wholeheartedly.

Cody's eyes shimmered with desire as he beckoned me closer. As I approached, he reached out, his firm hands drawing me into his arms. The moment our lips met, I sighed in ecstasy. During our heated exchange, Drew performed oral sex on Cody and me simultaneously.

Watching him strive to please us was an erotic sight. Cody's larger size filled his mouth, leaving barely enough room for me. Yet, Drew seemed determined, his efforts bringing waves of pleasure to us.

Turning to Cody, I smiled, my heart swelling with affection. His eyes sparkled in response, mirroring my smile. He leaned in, capturing my lips once again in a deep kiss. His tongue gently explored my mouth.

Drew patted the mattress, wanting us to join him on the bed.

In the dim light of the room, our naked bodies entwined as one. There was an unspoken understanding among us, a bond that transcended words. Cody and Drew took turns making love to me. To accommodate Drew's injuries, I straddled him. When it was Cody's turn, I laid on my back.

In these intimate moments, I shared kisses with both of them. We moved in rhythm, each touch deepening our connection. It was a moment of vulnerability, trust, and, most importantly, love.

* * *

I awoke with the evidence of our love-making still inside me. The intensity of our connection had been so powerful that we fell asleep afterward. Quietly slipping from the bed, I carefully wrapped a towel around myself before venturing out into the eerily hushed atmosphere of the bathhouse.

The horrifying realization that my husband had attempted to take my life weighed heavily on my mind. Resolute in my decision, I knew that once I returned home, I'd take steps to start divorce proceedings and secure a restraining order to protect myself from any further harm.

I entered the bathroom and sat down. In a matter of seconds, their combined fluids exited my body. Once finished, I wiped myself, feeling Cody's and Drew's touch still lingering. As I flushed the toilet, I sighed as their cum disappeared down the drain. I washed my hands and left the bathroom.

As I returned, I meandered aimlessly, not feeling tired. The tranquility of the bathhouse enveloped me, and the scent of eucalyptus brought a sense of peace.

Entering the "Fuck" room, I saw three men engaged in a fervent tryst. It was clear they were under the influence of some drug. The bottom was relentless, taking everything the tops gave him. He seemed to be in the throes of ecstasy.

Stepping away from the familiar, I entered the "Gloryhole" room. The dimly lit room featured partitions with waist-high circular openings, evoking a complex setting that was both suffocating and bewildering.

As I ventured forward, a man in the shadows stood motionless, his figure barely visible against the darkness. He seemed to blend seamlessly into the surroundings, almost like he was part of the room. His presence sent a shiver down my spine, and I hesitated, unsure what to do.

He gestured toward a gloryhole.

"I'm good," I responded tersely.

As I spun around, Brian, my husband, materialized before me like a ghost from the shadows. A gasp tore through me, shock rooting me to the spot at his sudden emergence. He grabbed me, his hands closing around me with a relentless, terrifying strength.

"What the fuck?" I shouted, completely thrown off by his presence.

"I have the knife. Scream, and you die right here."

A chill ran down my spine as I realized the gravity of his words. This was no nightmare. My husband wanted me dead.

I wriggled out of his grasp, plunging into the maze of gloryholes. I heard Brian call for help.

Moments later, the man wanting sex ran after me.

My heart pounded against my chest as the grim reality set in that this was Brian's lover. "Oh, God…" I whispered, the imminent threat of my demise looming over me.

While sprinting, I sought refuge behind a partition, my mind racing. I tried to stifle my gasps, but the fear made it impossible. I covered my mouth, praying my panicked breaths wouldn't give me away.

"Where the hell is he?" Brian's lover shouted, his voice echoing through the maze. "Why did you let him escape?"

"He slipped away! Find him, damn it!"

I crouched lower in the darkness, the pungent smell of semen assaulting my senses. How many men had found release here?

Their footsteps grew louder, approaching rapidly. I dropped to the floor, holding my breath as they rushed past. Once they were out of earshot, I crawled in the opposite direction, searching desperately for an exit sign. When it was nowhere to be found, despair washed over me, and I choked on a sob, knowing I might never make it out alive. The sound bounced off the walls, revealing my location.

"He's this way!" Brian's voice echoed menacingly.

Their footsteps rang out again, closer this time. In a rush of adrenaline, I sprang to my feet and bolted, eyes locking onto the glow of an exit sign. As I rounded the corner, Brian was there, waiting. His twisted smile confirmed my worst fears—he no longer loved me, and he wanted me dead.

I crashed into him, struggling to break free, but his accomplice was quick to pin me down. I cried out in fear, every heartbeat echoing the chilling reality of my situation.

They dragged me out of the "Gloryhole" room and down the hallway, forcing me into their room. After silencing me with a gag, they stripped me bare and tossed me onto the bed face-down. Moments later, they bound me to the steel posts in a grotesque, spread-eagle position. Helpless and on the verge of tears, I was at their mercy.

"What are we going to do?" Brian questioned.

His lover, a twisted grin on his face, revealed his eagerness for the torture he was about to unleash. I watched in horror as he pulled the menacing dildo from Brian's backpack.

"We're going to fuck him good!"

I gazed at Brian, my eyes begging him to reconsider, yet all that greeted me was his sinister grin. It was clear he relished my torment. Looking at his lover, I noticed he seemed to be about our age. Like Brian, he had a clean-shaven appearance. His hair was a mix of blond and reddish tones. However, what truly disturbed me was the crazed look in his eyes. That unhinged sparkle hinted at unspeakable acts.

Brian extracted the switchblade from his towel. With a swift flick of his wrist, it snapped open. The cold steel glinted menacingly in the dim light. Placing the sharp point against my cheek, he slowly dragged the blade down my face while muttering about how he was going to torture me.

I closed my eyes.

I tried to speak, but only muffled words escaped through the gag. Opening my eyes, I saw his cock throbbing with excitement.

"Fuck him, Damion..." Brian murmured. "Fuck him with the dildo. The little bitch needs to be put in his place."

His partner's name was Damion, and it suited him well. It was the name of someone evil. His cock measured about seven inches. It was the same size as mine—however, his dick head was enormous, mushroom-like. It could provide pleasure or a lot of pain.

I called out Brian's name, but my voice got muffled once again. Tears flowed from my eyes as Damion's fingers traced my body down to my ass. He slapped my cheeks hard, then spread them, looking at my fuck hole. Looking back, I could see him smiling. He enjoyed what he saw—my rosebud.

He started eating out my ass, moaning loudly from tasting the residue of jizz. His long tongue fucked me.

I shook my head, muttering, "No..."

Moments later, the horrifying ordeal unfolded, just as they had planned. Damion forcefully thrust the dildo inside me, moving it back and forth. I took the full 12-inches. The pain was intolerable.

"Pull it out." Brian directed.

Damion removed the dildo, crawling off the bed. He stood above me as they switched places, holding the 12-inch dong.

I gasped for breath as Brian started fucking me. He wasn't gentle. He was rough, and it excited Damion.

I closed my eyes as I felt the head of the dildo on my face. Thank God for the gag. Otherwise, I knew he'd choke me with it. Moments later, Brian moaned and came inside me. Damion took his turn and came quickly. Once his spasms stopped, he crawled off the bed and joined Brian. Exhausted from their brutal climax, they stood over me, grinning with perverse satisfaction.

As I lay there silently, I focused on their conversation, trying to decipher their next move. Although my ass throbbed with pain, the repeated sexual encounters over the weekend had numbed me, and I could bear it. Suddenly, I felt an itch on my chin. Instinctively, I moved it against the bed, and to my surprise, the gag in my mouth shifted slightly. I froze, fearful that they would notice if it fell out completely.

In forming a plan, I needed to be patient. I'd bide my time until I heard someone in the hallway. Then I'd remove the gag and scream for help. The key was timing. My heart pounded as I waited, the suspense consuming me.

* * *

As Brian and Damion conspired in hushed whispers, I waited in dread, tied to the bed. I could feel their malicious intent swirling around me like a dark cloud.

With a disturbingly calm manner, Brian approached me, and I could feel the cold metal of the knife as he traced its sharp edge against my skin, starting from the top of my back and moving down to my ass. This caused a wave of fear to wash over me, and an involuntary whimper escaped my lips. Instead of being deterred by my clear distress, Brian seemed to find a deeper, more sadistic pleasure.

For a heart-stopping moment, Brian's actions took a more menacing turn as he suddenly applied pressure, pressing the blade firmly against my skin. My mind raced, anticipating the searing pain of a cut, and I tensed every muscle in preparation for the imminent assault. However, he abruptly halted the pressure and withdrew the blade in an unexpected twist of mercy or perhaps a cruel extension of his game. As relief washed over me, a wave of unease followed closely behind, fueled by the uncertainty of his next move.

"Kill him now..." Damion muttered, his voice laced with impatience.

"Alright." Brian agreed, his tone nonchalant.

In a moment of sheer desperation, I turned toward Brian, my face contorted into a mask of pleading love. It was a last-ditch effort, a silent plea for mercy from someone I once trusted. My eyes searched his for any sign of the person I thought I knew, hoping he'd see reason, that the love we shared could somehow bring him back from the brink.

But his response was nothing short of chilling—a twisted grin spread slowly across his face as he raised the knife above me. It was a smile that spoke of malice and intent, sending shivers down my spine. I closed my eyes, waiting for the impending doom.

"Johnathan!" Cody yelled.

The sound of my name being called in the hallway was a beacon in the suffocating darkness. Seizing the momentary distraction, I dislodged the gag from my mouth by frantically rubbing it against the mattress. With newfound hope igniting within me, I screamed with all the strength I could muster.

Damion's response was instantaneous and filled with fury. "Shut him up!" he shouted, his voice a terrifying mix of panic and rage.

Brian lunged at me, trying to muffle my cries. But it was too late. The door crashed open, and Cody stormed in. Seeing the perilous situation, he lunged at Brian, holding the knife. Their struggle ensued, with the knife glinting dangerously in the air.

Cody cried out in pain as the knife sliced across his chest.

I strained against my bonds, but they wouldn't budge. Damion stood back, calculating and waiting for the right moment to strike. But Cody wasn't going down easily. With a powerful swing, he landed a punch on Brian's jaw, sending him sprawling to the floor.

Glinting under the dim light, the knife fell to Cody's feet.

I could see Damion creeping up behind him, silent and deadly, a predator closing in on his unsuspecting prey. Panic surged within me, compelling me to shout out a desperate warning. "Cody, watch out!"

Hearing my shout, Cody's reflexes kicked in. He bent down swiftly, his fingers closing around the knife. With a fluid motion, he swung around. The blade extended before him like a shield.

Damion, caught in the grip of his momentum, could not stop or swerve away in time. The scene seemed to unfold in slow motion as he impaled himself upon the sharp point of the knife. A look of shock and disbelief etched itself across his face.

For a moment, everything seemed to freeze. I held my breath, watching in horror as Damion staggered backward, a gurgling gasp escaping his lips. His eyes met mine, filled with a mix of pain and surprise, before he crumpled to the floor, his body hitting the cement with a dull thud that reverberated through the room.

"Untie me!" I demanded, frantic, to escape.

Cody hurried to my side, releasing me from my bonds.

I immediately rushed to Damion, kneeling beside his motionless body. His eyes were wide with disbelief, unable to fathom that he was the one dying, not me.

"Why?" I demanded, my voice echoing around the room. "Why?" I repeated, even though I knew I wouldn't get an answer. His eyes had turned into a frozen stare, looking back at me.

Cody gently pulled me away, holding me close.

"It's over..." he murmured, his voice a comforting whisper amidst the chaos.

I lifted my head as I heard footsteps echoing in our direction. It was Drew's voice, guiding someone toward us. He entered the room, followed by three police officers.

Still holding onto me, Cody extended his arm and pointed toward Brian, slowly regaining consciousness on the cold, unforgiving floor. An officer quickly moved toward Brian, snapping handcuffs around his wrists with a decisive click before pulling him up to stand on unsteady feet.

"Get him out of here!" I screamed, my voice raw with anger and fear. "That son-of-a-bitch tried to kill me!" My words echoed in the charged atmosphere.

As the officer pushed Brian out of the room, Brian turned his head to sneer at me. His eyes bore into mine with a look of pure disdain, a silent vow of revenge. It was a chilling moment that underscored the depth of his malice, even in defeat.

"Let's sit down," Cody whispered.

Drew came forward, and together they led me to the bed. We all sat down.

As an officer asked us questions, Drew pulled me in. His comforting presence made me feel secure and safe once again.

The distant wail of sirens signaled the paramedic's return. Before long, they arrived in the room. I recognized the handsome paramedic from earlier. He glanced at me briefly before his gaze fell on Cody. Their unspoken interest still lingered between them.

The paramedic addressed Cody's chest wound, cleaning and bandaging it with professional precision. As Cody's body responded to the medic's touch, his prick turned hard under the towel draped on his lap. The medic's eyes flicked back and forth between Cody's eyes and his arousal, a hint of desire seeping through his professional demeanor.

After the officers had concluded their questioning, meticulously documenting our harrowing experiences, they stepped aside. This allowed the medics to transfer Damion's motionless form onto a gurney. Covering his face with a sheet, this marked the end of his tumultuous existence.

When the officer mentioned that Cody would have to go to the station, I exchanged a glance with Drew. He nodded, understanding my thoughts. We'd go with him. I had to corroborate his story. He wasn't a murderer. Damion had impaled himself on the knife.

"Can I get dressed?" Cody asked, gesturing toward his naked body.

"Yes, of course," replied the officer.

"We'll meet you there," I said, grasping his hand.

Cody stood and turned toward me. "After this ends, I want you to come to my condo."

"Drew, also?"

"Of course…" He grinned and turned to the paramedic. "You're welcome to come, too!"

The paramedic's smile broadened. "I'm Reid," he stammered, lost in Cody's good looks.

When Cody stepped forward to shake his hand, the officer guided him out of the room. The cop cut short their introduction, leaving them with a lingering sense of unfinished conversation. However, their smiles warmed my heart. Everything was going to be alright, and this nightmare was soon to be over.

* * *

Several hours after we arrived at the police station, Reid appeared out of uniform. He introduced himself again and promptly joined our group. His physique was noticeably fit and muscular, a testament to his fitness commitment.

As we awaited Cody's release, our conversation flowed, allowing us to become acquainted with one another. He mentioned he was single, and then the conversation shifted toward Cody. He was attracted to him. I shared everything I knew, including our meeting this past weekend. Reid seemed like a sweet man. I could tell he was kind-hearted and genuinely a good person.

As our conversation lulled, the door swung open, and Cody appeared. We immediately rose to our feet, seeking clarity from him.

"Are you free to go?" I inquired.

He responded with a nod. "Let's get the hell out of here."

Reid, shaking off his nervousness, moved forward to offer his hand. Cody, however, skipped the handshake and went straight for a hug. As their eyes met, they shared a kiss. I let out a sigh, observing the immediate spark between them.

"Are you okay?" Drew asked me.

I turned and smiled. "I couldn't be happier."

After we were cleared to leave, we piled into Reid's Honda Pilot. It was spacious enough that we all fit comfortably without feeling cramped. With Drew's hand resting on my knee, I stayed quiet for most of the ride. He knew my mind was replaying the events of the evening.

We arrived at Cody's "First Hill" condominium. It was just a five-minute walk to downtown and the bustling, gay neighborhood of Capitol Hill. Modern pieces sparsely furnished his residence. He was a minimalist who liked organization and no clutter, creating a relaxing, stress-free environment.

Drew and I sat on the couch as Cody and Reid prepared a charcuterie board and got everyone refreshments. We chatted about everything that had happened. At one point, Cody looked at me in realization and sadness.

"I killed a man."

"He impaled himself on the knife," I murmured. My heart ached to see him in so much pain. "Oh, Cody... It wasn't your fault."

"I feel responsible."

"He wanted me dead."

Hearing the reality of the situation, he nodded his head.

I reached out and held his hand.

Reid grasped his shoulder, giving him support too.

Afterward, we all engaged in quiet, intimate conversations. Drew and I delved deeply into a discussion about our blossoming relationship. Our conversation flowed naturally, solidifying our longing for each other. I realized Drew was the man capable of fulfilling all my desires. In return, I felt confident I could reciprocate his love and commitment.

Looking up, I saw Reid unbuttoning Cody's shirt. Cody didn't object, letting him proceed. I looked at Drew, whispering that we should give them some privacy. Drew nodded, and we both stood to leave.

"Where are you going?" Cody asked.

"Back to the hotel."

"Please stay," Cody added a moment later.

"You don't want to be alone?"

"We want to be with you."

"All of us? Sexually?" I asked, trying to understand the situation.

Cody and Reid nodded.

I looked at Drew, who also nodded in agreement.

Cody assisted Reid in standing upright, their connection clear as they prepared to embrace this shared experience. As they began to undress, revealing their bodies, Drew and I mirrored their actions, our desires fueling the anticipation.

Drew's arousal was unmistakable as he stepped out of his jeans, his erect cock standing proudly before us. The pulsing desire in his eyes hinted at the passion to come. As we all stood exposed, Cody and Reid's bodies were a sight to behold, each unique in its beauty. Reid's impressive girth caught our attention, a promise of the pleasures ahead.

Reid and I settled onto the couch while Drew and Cody made love to us. We were two couples side by side, enjoying the passion of intimacy.

Drew's lovemaking was a testament to his understanding of my body. He knew exactly where to touch, when to slow down, and when to speed up. It was as if he could read my mind, anticipating my needs and desires before I fully realized them.

I reached out, tangling my fingers in his hair, as I pulled him closer. His tongue twisted with mine. With a final, powerful thrust, he pushed deep inside me, his body shaking with the force of his orgasm. His moans filled the room, mixing with mine as I followed suit, my release washing over me in a wave of pure ecstasy.

He collapsed on top of me, his body still trembling from the aftershocks of his climax. I held him tightly, thanking him for the pleasure he had given.

I turned to see Cody coming inside Reid. Their passion was heart-swelling, and I knew they'd be together forever.

Once Drew's breathing steadied, he gently extricated himself from my arms and stood up. He turned to Cody, extending an inviting hand. There was a moment of hesitation as Cody looked at Reid, seeking his permission. With a nod of approval, Reid motioned toward me. Seconds later, Cody was kneeling between my legs, his tongue lapping at the sticky remnants that leaked from me.

I let out a low moan, my eyes fluttering shut as waves of pleasure rippled through me. Drew and Reid stood above us, their hands intertwined as they watched their respective partners engage in an intimate act. Their appreciative gazes only heightened the erotic atmosphere, adding an extra layer of arousal to the already charged room.

"Make love to me!" I pleaded, pulling Cody toward me.

He rose to his feet.

His length pressed against my slick opening, and with a gentle push, he slid inside and started thrusting back and forth. As he moved, he leaned down to capture my lips in a passionate kiss.

My body opened up to him, welcoming his length and girth with unreserved eagerness.

Cody's movements were deliberate and controlled, his hips rolling in a rhythm that left me gasping for breath. His cock hit all the right spots, teasing my prostate. I could feel the pressure building up inside me, a clear sign I was on the brink of another orgasm.

With each thrust, I could feel him reaching deeper inside me, claiming me in the most intimate way possible. The sensation was intense yet incredibly satisfying. I clung onto him, my fingers digging into his back as I urged him to go faster.

And then, with a final, powerful thrust, he pushed deep inside me, his body shaking with the force of his orgasm. His moans filled the room, mixing with mine as I followed suit, my release splattering on my abdomen.

Cody's lovemaking was an experience like no other, a journey of pleasure and intimacy that left me breathless. As we lay there, spent and satisfied, I knew this was a moment I would cherish forever.

Drew's gaze shifted between Reid and me, a silent question hanging in the air. I understood his unspoken request and nodded my consent. "Of course," I breathed, patting the couch next to me as an invitation.

With a sigh of relief, Drew reclined onto the plush couch, lifting his legs invitingly. His eyes locked onto Reid's, silently beckoning him closer. As Reid moved to position himself between Drew's spread legs, my cock twitched with anticipation, stirred by the raw desire displayed before me.

The sight of Reid's impressive girth entering Drew was nothing short of breathtaking. The expression of pure ecstasy etched on Drew's face as he accommodated Reid was a testament to the intense pleasure coursing through him.

Reid began moving, his thrusts slow and deliberate. The sight was incredibly arousing.

Drew's hand wrapped around his cock, and he began jacking himself. His eyes were half-closed, lost in the waves of pleasure. The sight of Drew pleasuring himself while being taken by Reid was erotic. I looked at Cody, and he smiled, watching it unfold.

Suddenly, Drew's body tensed, and a cry escaped his lips as he climaxed. His seed spilled onto his chest, a hot, sticky testament to his pleasure. Yet, Reid didn't stop. He continued to thrust into Drew, prolonging his orgasm and coaxing more moans from his lips.

For another five minutes, Drew continued to endure Reid's relentless thrusts. His body shuddered with each stroke, his spent cock twitching with aftershocks. His moans grew louder, desperate, as Reid drove him closer to another peak.

With a final, potent thrust, Reid pushed himself deep within Drew. A low groan rumbled from his chest as he released his jizz deep inside him.

Exhausted, Reid rolled onto his back, his chest heaving as he struggled to catch his breath. His hand reached upwards, seeking the familiar touch of Cody. Responding to his silent plea, Cody moved toward him, lying beside him and enveloping him in a comforting embrace.

Simultaneously, I pulled Drew close, our bodies nestling together in the aftermath of our shared pleasure. The four of us lay there, spent and sated from our climaxes, basking in the afterglow of our collective intimacy.

* * *

Cody owned a California king-sized bed, which comfortably accommodated all of us. I awoke to find Cody's gaze on me. We rose, careful not to disturb our partners, and went to the kitchen. It was now dusk. We had slept for hours. The exhaustion from the bathhouse and the exhilaration of our lovemaking had taken its toll.

On the way out of the room, Cody opened a drawer and removed sweatpants and T-shirts for us to wear.

We dressed in the kitchen, and afterward, Cody set about brewing a pot of coffee while I perched on a stool beside the island.

I watched, memorizing every detail of him. He was so handsome. I knew he was a good man and felt blessed to have found him.

He poured two cups of coffee and sat down beside me. I smiled and took a sip of coffee. It was a dark roast, and it tasted delicious. I waited for him to speak, and when he did, he was full of compassion. The love he had for me was clear.

"I knew you were special the moment I met you," he whispered. "You've brought so much joy into my life in such a short time."

I leaned in and pressed my lips against his, feeling the warmth and tenderness of his kiss. As we pulled back, our eyes locked.

"Drew loves you," he said, his voice filled with sincerity.

I placed my hand on top of his. He turned his palm up, intertwining his fingers with mine. Our hands fit together perfectly, like two pieces of a puzzle. "I love him, too," I replied.

"That's good to hear."

"And I like Reid," I added.

Cody's smile widened. "I think I've found my soulmate," he whispered.

I returned his smile, feeling a sense of peace and contentment in his presence.

"It may not be easy for him, though..." he trailed off.

"Why do you say that?" I asked, concerned.

"The newspapers will report on my visit to the bathhouse. My sexuality will become public knowledge."

"Oh, yes..." After contemplating deeply, I replied, "Reid will stand by your side."

"I hope so... It's time for me to be honest with everyone," he admitted.

"I'll be here for you," I promised him.

"Thank you," he said gratefully.

We sat there in silence for a while, just savoring the moment. The aroma of coffee filled the kitchen and the soft glow of the setting sun streamed in through the window. It was peaceful.

Eventually, Cody broke the silence. "Want to go watch the sunset?" he asked, a soft smile playing on his lips.

I nodded, standing up from the stool. We walked out onto the porch, hand in hand. As we watched the sun dip below the horizon, painting the sky with hues of orange and pink, I knew everything would be okay. No matter what life threw at me, Cody would be my friend.

Drew and Reid surprised us from behind. They had wakened and entered the patio. We turned, smiling, and opened our arms to them. We all stood quietly, watching the last rays of the sunset. After it concluded, we gathered as a group and embraced each other warmly.

* * *

After leaving Cody's condominium, Drew checked out of his hotel and spent the night with me. We enjoyed a private, intimate dinner before heading back to my hotel. We spent the rest of our evening in bed, talking and caressing each other. The evening culminated in us making love, after which we both fell into a deep sleep, exhausted from our passionate encounter.

When I woke the next morning, I instinctively reached for Drew, pulling him closer. I felt the comforting warmth of his body against mine. I gently kissed his head, content to stay in this position until we caught our flight back to San Francisco.

My arousal awakened him as it pressed against his ass. Drew turned over, greeting me with a sleepy smile.

"Good morning!" he whispered, voice still heavy with sleep.

"Hi!" I responded.

His arousal matched mine. Reaching down, I gently caressed him. As he throbbed in my hand, I knew we had just enough time for intimacy before heading to the airport.

"Do you want me to make love to you?" I asked, grinding my hips into him.

He nodded and reached for the packet of lube on the nightstand. After preparing me, he turned over and guided me into him.

I took my time, ensuring he could feel every inch of me. The sensation of his hole around me was incredible. "I won't last long," I warned.

"Don't hold back," he whispered.

With that, I increased my pace and soon reached my climax, releasing deep within him. I stayed inside as he pleasured himself, and his release stained the bed sheets. Afterward, I held him close before we got up to shower.

As Drew bathed, I called Matteo to say goodbye. We had a wonderful chat in which he expressed his friendship with me. We exchanged addresses, promising to stay in touch. Just as I was about to end the call, Matteo interjected. He explained he had told Ciro about what happened at the bathhouse and wasn't upset.

"Johnathan, he made love to me last night. I'm so happy..." Matteo shared, his voice filled with joy.

I smiled at his cheerful demeanor. "I'm so happy for you."

"Si, me too!" he replied.

With that, we said our goodbyes, and I joined Drew in the shower. I bathed him, and then he bathed me.

* * *

The skies had brightened beautifully. Sunlight bathed us, yet a crisp coolness was present as we departed from the hotel and made our way toward Westlake station. We boarded the light rail—Seattle's transport system to the airport. We secured a couple of seats by the window. Drew, absorbed in his phone, paid no attention to his surroundings, allowing me to gaze out the window and reflect on the weekend's events.

My reckless decisions led me into frightening situations, but I didn't berate myself for any of them. What I'd experienced was necessary—it had strengthened me and taught me valuable lessons. I turned to look at Drew and realized that my days of seeking anonymous intimacy were over. I was content with the love of one man.

When he looked up and saw me staring, he returned my smile. Leaning forward, he kissed me, unbothered by the prying eyes of the commuters. My heart swelled with anticipation of what lay ahead, knowing I had someone by my side who truly loved me.

The End

Acknowledgments

I extend my heartfelt thanks to the remarkable people who helped craft this story—their contributions have been invaluable. A special acknowledgment goes to my friend Logan Zachary, whose steadfast advice and insight helped to shape this narrative. I'm also indebted to Zakery Leigh, a truly exceptional artist, for creating a stunning book cover. And, of course, my deepest gratitude to you, the reader, for your encouragement and support.

About the Author

Hailing from the Pacific Northwest, Franco De Rocco is an esteemed writer and painter who has captivated a global audience with his skill in crafting intricate and compelling narratives, earning him numerous accolades. Franco's artistic prowess enhances his writing, lending a unique visual dimension. Beyond his creative pursuits, he is a devoted family man, cherishing his roles as a husband and stepfather to his two extraordinary sons. His family is completed by two beloved golden retrievers who hold a special place in his heart.

For more information about Franco, please visit his website at www.FrancoDeRocco.com.

Books by Author

Rise of the Queer Vampires

Immerse yourself in the alluring realm of Rise of the Queer Vampires, a fresh take on gay erotic fiction. The narrative centers around Antonio de Luca, an Italian youth grappling with his sexual orientation amidst the strict moral codes of his Catholic upbringing. His search for temporary comfort leads him to anonymous sexual encounters, providing fleeting moments of liberation.

However, Antonio's life veers off its usual course one fateful evening when he crosses paths with a mysterious stranger who transforms him into a vampire. This sudden and dramatic change propels Antonio on a heart-stopping journey filled with danger, self-discovery, and an unquenchable thirst—for blood and love.

Rise of the Queer Vampires weaves together sensuality, danger, and suspense, crafting a tale that is as titillating as it is thrilling. The story is brimming with an erotic energy that will ignite your imagination and bring your fantasies to life.